ALSO BY KATI WILDE

KATI WILDE

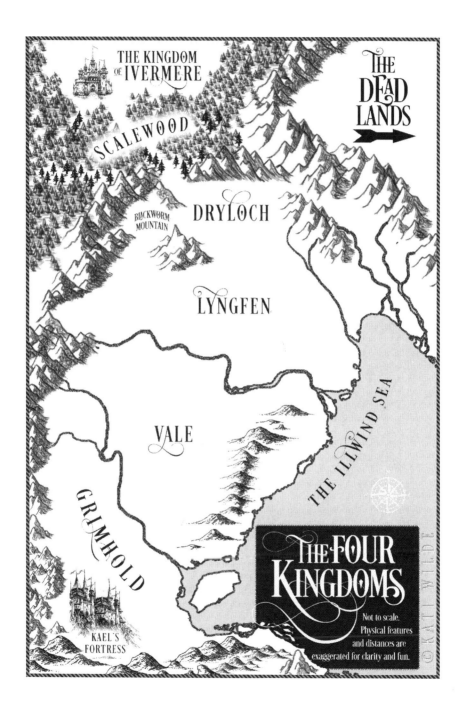

THE KINGDOM OF IVERMERE

THE DEAD LANDS

SCALEWOOD

DRYLOCH

BLACKWORM MOUNTAIN

LYNGFEN

VALE

THE ILLWIND SEA

GRIMHOLD

KAEL'S FORTRESS

THE FOUR KINGDOMS

Not to scale.
Physical features
and distances are
exaggerated for clarity and fun.

© KATI WILDE

HERE WE ARE, AT THE *last of four tales about brides who travel great distances drawn by hope, or driven by fear, and who find happiness in the arms of an alien, and a wolf, and a billionaire.*

Now comes the warlord king.

The time is anotherwhen, a date unknown but in the midst of winter; the place is anotherwhere, a world unnamed but to the west of the Illwind Sea. And this story begins, as many stories do, with a lonely warrior wandering through a fortress guarded by mighty walls that are as thick and as hard as the walls around his heart. Surely only a brave bride—or a very desperate one—could scale those stone battlements...or any of the other thick and hard parts of him.

So we settle in for a midwinter's spell—for that is all a tale is, words woven together in hopes of making magic. It matters not if you believe in such things. You must only believe this—

Love is magic, too.

1

KAEL THE BUTCHERER

Grimhold

KAEL STRODE INTO THE CHAMBER that ought to have been filled with shackled prisoners and the beseeching cries of the penitent—and found it disappointingly empty. Frowning, he turned to the sentry posted beside the chamber doors. "Is this not the petition hall?"

The young guard's only response was the metallic shivering of chainmail and a panicked hiss of breath.

If Kael asked the simple question again the boy might piss himself in fear. Frustration gritted his teeth. A flash of blue farther down the corridor caught his eye—one of the royal underministers, a woman he'd seen cowering in the great hall during his endless meetings with his advisors. "You there!"

The figure froze. A timid, "Yes, your majesty?" floated toward him.

"Is this not the petition hall?"

Though the underminister had the courage to approach him, she was trembling as hard as the sentry—but silently trembling, for her woolen robes didn't jingle. "It is, sir."

Just as Kael had thought. "Then is it not Petition Day?"

In each of his four kingdoms, anyone sentenced by local magistrates or whose complaints were unresolved had a right to petition the king for a hearing. Kael had only recently learned that a high magistrate had been overseeing the hearings in the petition hall each month, as had been established during Geofry's reign.

Kael enjoyed few royal duties. It seemed that his every hour was filled with tedious meetings and pointless rituals. But he had looked forward to this day, when he might hear how his kingdoms' laws were applied—and learned which of Geofry's still needed to be struck down.

"It is," she answered.

"Why is no one here, then?"

Her cheeks paled and she bit her lip. Her gaze darted to the sentry, as if searching for help, but the boy could hardly breathe let alone give Kael an explanation.

The underminister attempted it. "Because…I have heard…that is…" In a sudden rush, she got it out— "There *are* no petitioners."

Kael's frown deepened. "No petitioners?" He had

seen previous dockets. Each month brought dozens of petitions. "Why?"

Mutely she stared at him.

Curse every breath that Geofry ever took. So frightened was she, Kael would have to pull her tongue from her mouth to get an answer from it—as Geofry had done in truth to those who'd said words he hadn't wanted to hear. Too many silent servants roamed these stone corridors to wonder at her fear now.

If Kael wanted an answer, he would have to seek it elsewhere.

It finally came, however, from an unexpected direction. "The prisoners learned that you would deliver the new rulings, sir," the sentry told him, voice little more than a squeak. "And decided to accept the sentences they'd received."

Rather than risk worse from him? More fools they. Kael had been in a fine mood this day. *Had* been.

What his mood looked like now, Kael could not say, except that after braving another glance at his face, the underminister's fingers shook ever harder as she pointed down the stone corridor in the direction from which she'd come. "I believe you are expected in the great hall instead, your majesty."

Where a large number of people had gathered, Kael concluded by the noise coming from that chamber as he approached. And this was what becoming a king had made him—for many years he had been called Kael the

Conqueror, yet at this moment he dreamt of finding a cupboard to hide in. Anything to avoid more royal pageantry.

His sour mood worsened when he stepped into the great hall and saw the cushion of woven flowers blanketing the golden seat of his throne. Over a year ago, he'd told the ladies of the court not to waste time on such frivolities.

He would not tell them again. Without a word, Kael drew his sword. The courtiers and servants within the opulent marble chamber abruptly fell silent. Some trembled and stumbled out of his path, but he paid them no mind. His grim gaze was fixed on the white roses as he stalked toward the dais.

From his left approached a scurrying figure in red silken robes and cap. Lord Minam, his royal chamberlain, scurried everywhere—as a mouse did. Or as a thief did.

Kael admired both thieves and mice. More than any other class of man or animal, they were likely to survive a calamity. Which was probably why Minam had so well survived the eighteen months since Kael had taken the throne.

And it was probably why Minam had survived the king who'd sat on it before him. Kael had never dreamed of ruling one kingdom, let alone four. But if ever there was a man who'd begged for a length of sharpened steel down his gullet, Geofry the Child-Eater was he—and Kael had always been generous with his blade. His steel had given Geofry's gullet, balls, and brains a skewering before he was done.

Kael hadn't intended to win Geofry's crown in the killing. Yet win it, he had.

"My king," the chamberlain came up alongside him, scurrying even faster now to keep up with Kael's longer stride, and the lilting rhythm of all the four kingdoms in his voice. Even after so many years among them, to Kael's ears their speech still sounded like a song. "With my own eyes, I inspected your cushion. This time it is free of thorns."

"I care nothing of thorns." Of all the things that had ever poked Kael's ass, the least painful was a flower. "I care that anyone in this castle wastes time weaving unwanted cushions."

"It is only because Geofry—"

"Wanted his ass perfumed?" With a sneer, Kael slipped the flat of his blade beneath the woven flowers and tossed the cushion to the marble floor. "More pleasant for you all to kiss it."

Rare steel replaced the placating cadence of the chamberlain's voice. "When Geofry ordered us to kiss it, my king, he would first sit in the blood of our wives and children."

For that—and worse—Kael had destroyed him. So he replied with steel of his own, but his was hotter than the chamberlain's. "I am *not* Geofry." Yet still he was treated as Geofry had been. "I have no need to be coddled and flattered, or to sit upon a perfumed cushion."

Minam sighed. "But that is what a king does, my liege."

That is what a king does. In the past year and a half, Kael had learned to hate those words. For a king spent every day upholding the laws of the kingdom and protecting his people—not by his own sword, but by sitting on a pillow and consulting a parade of advisors, ministers, and officials. From the moment he woke until his despairing fall into sleep, it seemed Kael spent every day petted and led and fed, living more like a cow being fatted for slaughter than a king.

When Kael gave no reply, the chamberlain sighed again and bent to lift the blanket of flowers. "It took great effort to cultivate roses so near to Midwinter. The ladies only wish to please you."

No. They only wished to appease him. As he sheathed his sword, Kael could see the women's frightened gazes shifting from the cushion to his face. As if they expected Kael to behead them for growing and weaving the flowers.

He wouldn't behead anyone. Not for such a paltry offense as that.

Still, seeing their fear fanned the frustration that had smoldered in his heart for the better part of his rule. He snatched the cushion from Minam's grip and flung it into the center of the chamber.

"If you wish to please me, then spend your days weaving blankets for the children maimed by your putrid king! Waste them not with this foolishness!" Petals fluttered through the air as he bellowed, "And if you do not have business here, begone from my sight!"

A rush of sandals and silks followed. Heavily Kael sat upon the gold throne and immediately wished himself anywhere else. Geofry had been a tall man, a strong warrior, and this seat had been made for the Child-Eater.

It had not been made for a man of Kael the Conqueror's great size, and he felt confined—imprisoned—in its golden clasp.

Yet he had not yet decided what to do with it. Gladly would he melt it into coins and distribute them throughout the kingdoms, but even a team of oxen could not drag the heavy gold throne from atop the marble dais where it stood. And the people of the four kingdoms—*his* people—seemed reassured by Kael inhabiting Geofry's seat.

Hanging Geofry's eviscerated and headless carcass from the fortress wall ought to have reassured them well enough, so that was the first thing Kael had done. Except not a day had passed before a mob had torn what was left of Geofry down, carried the corpse across the bridge to the center of the city, and burned it atop a bonfire. When the pyre finally cooled, they pissed in the ashes.

Kael had known they were truly his people then—but he still could not fathom why they had made him their king.

He still could not fathom why he had accepted.

"Your crown, my liege." With a flourish, Minam presented the bejeweled circlet of gold nestled on a purple velvet pillow.

Gritting his teeth, Kael took the crown. This bauble

fit no better than the throne did. Perched atop his head, it threatened to slide off with every nod. But his people were also reassured by seeing it—and Minam claimed that for official tasks it conveyed the proper authority.

Kael thought that any king who could not convey authority without a crown was not much of a king at all. But whatever reason they were gathered here, he must be needed to—

What reason *were* they gathered? Only the more fainthearted courtiers had fled at his command. At least fifty remained—which meant they believed they had business here.

Scowling, he looked to Minam. "What foolishness is…"

He was speaking to himself. The chamberlain stood a few steps away, engaged in a hectic, whispered conversation with the Minister of Wards. Their heads were bent together, the chamberlain's red silk cap against the minister's white, and Minam's pale hands moved in short, agitated gestures as he spoke to the conjurer.

The Minister of Wards was the only spellcaster within the stronghold, and his single duty was to maintain the wards that shielded those living in the fortress from corrupt magic. Twice every day he solemnly reported to Kael that all of his runes were intact. As he had made that morning's report only two hours ago, Kael doubted any magical disaster had occurred in that time.

Abruptly both men seemed to sense the weight of their king's gaze upon them. They fell silent and turned to face him—Minam's expression as innocent as any thief who had been caught with his hand in a sack of gold, and the minister's eyes anxiously rounded, mouth pulled into a taut, pained smile.

Kael knew scheming when he saw it, and his fine mood returned. "Have you gathered to kill me, then?" With a sweep of his hand, he indicated the crowd. "Are you all carrying daggers to plunge into my heart?"

Such an attempt would surely be more entertaining than whatever Minam had been truly whispering about.

Expression aghast, Minam scurried back to Kael's side. "You are our liberator, my liege! Never would we—"

"Then what perverted plot sends Lord Apel slinking away like a guilty jackal?" He indicated the minister, who was darting through the crowd. "Does he intend to use his magics to shrink me to the size of a flea? I warn you now, he will fail. I will be the size of a pig, at least."

As if finally recognizing Kael's teasing, the chamberlain's tension eased. "Nothing of the sort. We have a guest, sir, and Lord Apel was uncertain whether the wards in her quarters would be strong enough."

Kael frowned, his amusement gone. "A spellcaster visits?"

One more powerful than the minister? Lord Apel hailed from one of the high families of Ivermere, and few people possessed stronger magic than that realm's nobility did.

"Yes, my king."

Kael's eyes narrowed. "An *unexpected* guest?"

He had hoped for a distraction in his royal routine, but a threat would not offer much of one. If this sorceress had foul intentions, he would destroy her before she could harm anyone under his protection.

"We expected her," the chamberlain assured him, only to add, "though we did not expect her *this* day. And we did not know *who* she would be, or even if she would *ever* be—"

Kael's deep frown brought the chamberlain's confused ramblings to an abrupt halt. "Who is she?"

Was she a danger to his people?

The chamberlain lifted his chin. "Your bride, sir."

"My bride?" Kael echoed.

"Your bride," said Minam again, as if the problem lay in Kael's ears and not in the sparse sense coming from his own mouth. "She arrived only an hour past."

"My *bride* did."

"Yes, my king."

Bemused, Kael asked, "How long have I had a bride, Minam?"

A wry smile pulled at the chamberlain's mouth. "For an hour, sir."

Kael's shout of laughter turned every head within the chamber, fifty pairs of wary eyes settling on him. That was not a sound they often heard from their king—nor was his wide grin a sight familiar to them.

By the gods, Kael had wanted a distraction and he had surely been granted one. "So you are not here to kill me, but to chain some unfortunate woman to my side?"

Smile vanishing, Minam insisted indignantly, "It is no misfortune to marry you, my king."

That was probably how Minam had enticed her to agree—promising great fortune. Still, she must be brave. Or a madwoman. Or both.

Now he was intrigued. "Who is she?"

Proudly Minam announced, "She is Anja of Ivermere, eldest daughter of King Palin and Queen Dena. We have gathered here so that she might be presented to you... but there has been a complication."

Kael was unsurprised to hear it. "She has decided not to sacrifice herself on the dark altar of my bed?"

The color in Minam's face deepened until it matched the red silk of his cap. For Kael referred to the nights—and days—after he had killed Geofry and been named king, when the ladies of the court had shown him so much appreciation and rewarded him so well that he had not left his bedchamber for a full week.

Until he had overheard whispers that the ladies disguised their fear and faked their pleasure—and had only attended to him in hopes of keeping their new king so sated that he would not drag the young and innocent girls of his kingdoms into his bed.

Kael had not touched a woman since. He wanted no one who only kissed him out of duty or in fear—whether that terror was for herself or for someone else—or who felt she had no choice but to please her king. He was *not*

Geofry…or any of the other tyrants in his past whom he
had known and slaughtered.

"Princess Anja is willing, my liege, but currently—"

Willing. In an instant, Kael leapt from the prison
of his throne, striding purposefully through the crowd.
"Where is she?"

Scurrying after him, Minam replied, "Perhaps you
should first visit your chambers to choose finer raiment,
your majesty."

Kael didn't bother with an answer to that. They would
truss him up like a roasted goose, then paste on the feathers.
He preferred the easy movement of his loose tunic and
leather breeches.

The chamberlain sighed. "Perhaps the princess will
think you were too eager to meet her to dress properly."

Then the princess would think rightly. "Where is she?"
Kael asked again, this time not so patiently.

"In the warded quarters, but—"

"Where are the warded quarters?" The ancient king
who built this mountain stronghold had included so
many chambers, corridors, and stairs that any invader
who managed to breach the battlements would be fated
to wander, lost and despairing, until they succumbed to
slow starvation. Only now it was Kael who might become
lost within the maze of his fortress. Knowing a thousand
unimportant words would precede the chamberlain's
answer, however, Kael pointed to a serving girl who was
waiting on the courtiers, tray in hand. "You there! Show

me the way to my bride!"

The tray clattered to the floor. The girl moved with such haste that even Kael was forced to quicken his long strides to keep her in sight.

The chamberlain puffed along beside him. "Your majesty—"

"From Ivermere, you said?" And a powerful sorceress if she hailed from the royal family, but she would soon learn the four kingdoms had little use for her corrupt magics. "Did you intend to strengthen the ties between our kingdoms? That is well done."

"I cannot take such credit, my king," Minam huffed as they raced up a stairwell, "for I didn't know *who* would come in answer to our royal missives proclaiming that we had a king in need of a queen."

"Whose royal missives?" Kael had not put his seal to any such missives.

"Letters were sent under my seal to every kingdom in every direction, my liege."

"And this princess arrived first because she is nearest?" Only a forest separated Ivermere from Dryloch, his northernmost kingdom.

"No, my liege. We sent the first letters last summer, shortly after your abstinence began." The red still had not left Minam's face, but whether it was the effort of keeping up with the servant girl or the effort of conveying this information, Kael didn't know. "I feared for your health, for a man with a constitution as, er…a constitution as…"

"Primitive?"

"With a constitution as *passionate* as yours to go so long without, er—"

"Fucking?"

"—without *companionship*, my king. But when our inquiries within the four kingdoms received no response, we posted to the four winds and to all the outward kingdoms."

"You never thought to inform me that a bride might arrive?"

"I feared raising your hopes, sir. In truth, I despaired there would never be an answer, for many are frightened by your reputation—"

"As a ruthless butcherer?" A well-earned reputation.

The chamberlain appeared offended. "People within the other kingdoms do not know your heart as I do. And, as I know you have no great love for spellcasters, I initially sent no message to Ivermere at all. But when there was no answer from the rest of the world…"

He had been desperate enough to risk his king's wrath.

But Kael felt no anger. The chamberlain clearly believed that Kael's sullen frustration stemmed from his abstinence, not his irritation with the duties of a king. Or perhaps Minam well knew the truth of the matter, and of Kael's ill-content. Whether to serve Kael or serve the people, Minam meant to ease his king's unhappiness.

And taking a bride was not such a terrible thought. A princess would be familiar with Kael's royal duties and share in them—and Kael might have warm arms and a warmer cunt to look forward to at the end of the tedious parade of meetings each day.

Ahead, the girl was still running down the stone corridor, passing beneath an archway marked by a faintly glowing rune—

"Halt!" Kael bellowed and the girl skidded to a stop, looking fearfully back. He reached her side and said, "If a spellcaster resides within, do not pass the wards without first announcing yourself. Just as in a healer's square. You understand?"

Eyes wide, the girl nodded.

"Begone, then," he told her gently, and as she raced away, he said to Minam, "Every servant and courtier within the fortress will need to be reminded of this. Put a sentry at this spot to warn everyone who passes this way."

"It will be done."

Kael frowned as the chamberlain continued with him. "You should also remain behind."

"If you will risk her magic, sir, then so will I," Minam replied bravely, then added, "Each of the chambers and walls within this wing are also warded."

Providing layers of shielding until they reached the same room as the princess—or any other of her party. Everyone born in Ivermere was a spellcaster, though of varying talents. Kael thought it better that they didn't use magic at all while in his kingdoms, but he had never known anyone from Ivermere who did not resort to a spell for the most trivial of matters. In all likelihood, his bride could not even get undressed without magic.

It didn't matter if she couldn't. He would undress her, instead.

The warded quarters were similar to the king's private quarters, though not as great in scope. There were dining chambers and sitting rooms and parlors aplenty—all of which he expected to be filled with courtiers and attendants, as surely befitted a princess's wedding party.

But perhaps he was mistaken. For certain he had never *seen* a princess's wedding party. But as he could not even visit the nearby city without half the fortress's residents accompanying him—for that was what a king did—Kael assumed the same was true of a princess. He frowned as they passed through yet another empty chamber. "How many from the Ivermere court accompanied her?"

"Only Lord Eafen, who is their Minister of Foreign Concerns, and three dozen soldiers." Minam cleared his throat. "Lord Eafen has requested that we provide ladies-in-waiting to attend to the princess, which we have."

So that she could ready herself? "Is that the complication? Her hair is undone?"

Minam hesitated before answering, "Not *precisely*, my king."

Not precisely, because as they entered the next chamber and discovered a cluster of ladies hovering outside the entrance to a sitting chamber, it was apparent that they had not ventured beyond the next ward to help the princess fix her hair. It was not the princess's magic they feared, however.

It was her sword.

Kael's steps slowed as the ladies barring his path scrambled out of the way, allowing him a full view into the next chamber.

For the barest moment he thought the figure standing atop the lounging sofa could not be the princess, for her hair was not only undone, but as white as a crone's—not a pale blonde, for there wasn't a hint of gold, but a snowy white that tumbled down her back in thick waves. She faced away from Kael, her sword gripped in both hands and the blade angled out in front of her. Slowly she turned—following the slow path of a tall, dark-haired man wearing a finely embroidered tunic and a cajoling expression that matched the voice he was using to urge her down. Surrounding them in a wide circle were soldiers—though none of them with weapons drawn, and all of them looking helpless.

She was keeping the Ivermeren minister and soldiers at bay, Kael realized. Not attacking them, but defending herself—like a cat that had climbed atop a safe perch and swiped at anything that came too near.

Abruptly she shook her head and shouted at the minister, "Listen to me, you dogbrained fool! You will return me home *now!*"

Grimly, Kael said to Minam, "Willing, you say?"

"I swear it, my king! She has told me herself that she wishes to marry you. This is regarding another matter—she believes her mother is in danger." The chamberlain barely paused for a breath before adding, "See how fierce she is? Does she not suit you? A man of your past cannot be content with a woman who easily submits. You surely long for a woman who must be conquered."

A man of his past knew that a body could be conquered—but that a heart must be won.

But winning that fiery heart *would* be a challenge. And winning the body would be a pleasure, Kael decided, particularly now that he could see more of it.

Everyone could see more of it. Not only was her hair unbound, but she was clad in a white sleeping robe, its belt hanging open and the collar sliding down one pale shoulder. Beneath the robe was a silken red nightgown that clung to the swell of her breasts and the curve of her waist. As the princess turned, she weaved unsteadily, and when she suddenly shook her head again, it was not in denial as he'd thought before—but as if attempting to clear her mind.

Had she just risen from bed, though the sun was high overhead? And was she *drunk*?

Already Kael liked this bride. Very much.

His gaze never leaving the princess, he told Minam, "If any other brides answer the summons, send them away. I will take this one."

In a voice faint with relief, Minam answered, "Yes, my king."

"Stay behind the ward," he warned the chamberlain

before striding forward into the sitting chamber. Some of
the soldiers were gesturing uncertainly at each other, as if
half-heartedly developing some idiotic plan to knock the
princess from her perch and take her sword—and cover
her mouth to prevent her from chanting any spells, which
would make her far more dangerous than her blade, even
against these other spellcasters.

Strange that she wielded a sword at all. Sorcerers rarely
did, preferring instead to attack with spells.

Let her. Kael did not fear magic. "Princess Anja."

Her robe flared around her legs as she spun to face him.

He ought not be surprised that she was beautiful. Every
spellcaster he'd ever met used their magic to reshape their
appearance. Yet the current trend among sorcerers was
a high forehead and large, rounded eyes set amidst thin
and delicate features. But he *was* surprised, because she
had not adhered to the current fashion, and her beauty
was not only in her features but the way she looked upon
him, proud and fearless. It seemed that every aspect of
her face was designed to strike at his senses, to please and
defy and arouse him—from the wide fullness of her lips
to the imperious lift of her chin and the dark eyebrows
arched above her narrowed, challenging stare.

Entranced by her bold beauty, Kael did not halt until
the point of her blade met his chest—and then pressed
closer. Immediately she relaxed her wrists, as he'd assumed
she would, because if she had wished to harm anyone she
would have been chanting a spell. But she had already

told the minister what she wanted.

Listen to me.

She abruptly frowned, then wavered again on her feet before steadying herself, blade held between them. "It is *you!*"

"It is me," Kael agreed, carefully watching her swaying frame. "Though you have come to marry me, you seem unhappy to see me. What upsets you, princess? Am I not handsome enough?"

"You are more handsome than you should be, brute. But I do not like that you are even bigger than is rumored," she told him, and the waft of her breath was not laden with mead or wine, but another scent that reminded him of a mulled cider—cinnamon and cloves and apple. Yet whatever she'd imbibed must have been potent, for he could see the flush in her cheeks and hear the slurring of her tongue. She drew the blade away, keeping hold of the hilt with one hand and reaching toward him with the other. Her assessing gaze ran down his length, and her fingers gripped his biceps, squeezing the thick muscle through his linen sleeve. "Stronger, too, I think."

By the gods, he prayed that she would be willing *tonight.* Such fire spread from her touch that he was instantly aflame.

"You are tall enough to take me," he rasped softly. Standing atop the lounging sofa gave her additional height, yet she would have been tall without it. Her long legs would wrap around his waist and hold him tight as he pumped between her thighs. "Strong enough, too."

For although she was slender, her arms were finely muscled—and she had no difficulty holding a heavy long-sword one-handed. Again, unusual for a sorceress. Some of the Ivermeren soldiers appeared softer than she did.

"Perhaps I am." She tilted her head, her full lower lip jutting out. Disappointment filled her voice as she said, "But you will not be easy to kill."

He grinned. "Did you hope I would be?"

"I did," she said, swaying toward him before catching herself. Gaze drawn to the luscious pout of her mouth, Kael ignored the agitated denials bursting from the Ivermeren minister. Her forefinger jabbed into his chest. "You are a ravening monster. Your sword hungers for blood and you rapaciously seek new kingdoms to conquer. Such a man cannot be long for this life. So I was certain that within a year you would be dead."

Laughing now, Kael asked, "You would give me a year of marriage, though?"

He would take it.

She fisted her hand in his tunic and dragged him close enough to kiss. Instead of touching her lips to his, she said fiercely, "After a year, surely you would torture and kill *me* when I do not use sorcery to further your bloody campaigns."

He would cherish her all the more for her refusal. And she was a powerful sorceress, indeed. No enchantment could bind a heart to another, yet she was already weaving a spell around his. Laughter fading, he told her softly, "I have no thought of killing you."

Torturing her was another matter. But it would be sweet torture, he could promise her that.

"Because I will kill you first," she vowed and pushed away, lifting her chin. "Perhaps while we are in bed and your throat vulnerable to a knife."

Kael would welcome her attempt. Her blood clearly burned as hot as his. They would battle between the furs and find their pleasure at the same time. "Will this attack come on our wedding night?"

Her brow creased as she contemplated her answer. Finally she decided, "After we have made an heir, so I never have to marry again." She swayed and this time the sword fell from her grip. For balance she clutched at his shoulders and leaned closer, her dark eyes locked with his. "But before I marry at all, I must return to Ivermere."

Kael could hardly tear his mind away from a vision of his bride with swollen belly, carrying their heir. So much seed would he spill within her, it would not be long before her knife was at this throat. A delay seemed intolerable. "Why must you return?"

"To kill a spider in the queen's bedchamber."

"A spider?"

"A *big* spider," she told him, and the mulled spices upon her breath heated every remaining inch of his skin that was not already burning. "As big as a cat. It has woven a web in the corner of the ceiling, high above her bed."

An exasperated sigh came from his right. "Your majesty, please understand that we have already found an errant spider in the queen's quarters and smashed—"

A single quelling glance from Kael halted the minister's words. "Your princess believes otherwise."

She drew his gaze again. "Because *they* do not see it. Only I do. Yet *they* thought it was only a virgin's nerves and sent me here. But I had no doubts. I have every intention of marrying you and killing you."

So he could see. But even the boldest sorceress would not announce her plans as she had. He might have thought it a joke…but for that spiced fragrance upon her breath. A grim suspicion of what it was began to enter Kael's mind.

Her imploring gaze searched his face. "Will you help me return to Ivermere and save my mother?"

With another sharp glance, Kael silenced the minister's protestations that started in response to her plea. To her, he vowed, "I will."

Her eyes narrowed again. "Should I trust Kael the Conqueror's word? Do you swear it?"

"I do." He caught her waist when she swayed again. "Now tell me what it was you most recently drank."

She blinked. "Only water. I was so very thirsty when I awoke."

And hungry. Her stomach gave a low growl that rumbled against the fingers spanning her waist.

Immediately he swept her into his arms and swung to face Ivermere's minister. As if dizzied by the movement,

Anja clung to his neck, resting her head against his shoulder and closing her eyes.

Unlike his princess, Lord Eafen had reshaped his face. He wore a nose so thin and a mouth so small that it appeared as if they were sinking into his skull and pushing out his rounded eyes to make room for themselves.

But there must be plenty of room in that head, because for certain there was no brain in it.

"You gave her the kissing potion," Kael said flatly.

Which had earned its name because the potion caused such a deep sleep that, for days or weeks, the sleeper did not eat or drink. So another person would give them sustenance by placing their lips together, filling the sleeper's mouth with water or broth, and coaxing them to swallow. But there were darker reasons for the name—that sometimes when women awoke, they were with a child they had no memory of conceiving.

"The queen gave it to her," the minister explained. "The princess announced that she was leaving to marry you, and almost immediately began making claims about this spider. Our queen believed her delay betrayed a bride's doubts and gave Princess Anja the potion, so that she might undergo the journey in a calm manner."

Kael thought Queen Dena deserved whatever the spider in her room might do to her. "Was the princess touched while sleeping?"

Nervously the minister wrung his thin hands. "She is still a virgin—"

"I don't care if she is!" Kael roared. If he had not been cradling his bride against his chest, then his sword would have been cleaving through the minister's and soldiers' necks. "Was she touched *without her knowing?*"

"No, your majesty! Even for water and broth, we used a cup and helped her sip, and the female soldiers attended to her sleeping form. We would not betray her in that way!"

But they *had* betrayed her. First her mother, then this minister, then the soldiers. "Begone from my kingdoms," he said softly. "Flee north to Ivermere as if the Butcherer of the Dead Lands rides close behind, because I promise you—if you or your soldiers tarry even a moment, I *will* be."

The minister's face blanched. "Your majesty—"

"BEGONE!"

Kael did not wait to watch them obey. Rage pounding through his veins, he strode across the sitting room with Anja in his arms. To the ladies hovering outside the door, he barked, "See that she is brought something to eat. *Now!*"

She had likely not consumed anything substantial in almost three weeks—the length of the carriage journey from Ivermere to his stronghold. The ladies fled, and he looked to Minam, who was flitting about anxiously.

"Lead me to her bedchamber," Kael commanded.

Minam scurried ahead.

"You were unkind to that toad," Anja murmured against his neck, her voice heavy with exhaustion—probably the lingering effects of the potion. Her truth-telling had probably been, too.

Kael needed no potion to tell the truth. "He deserved worse."

"He only did what he was ordered to do," she said.

"Not what *you* ordered him to do."

This time he heard the smile in her reply. "I cannot blame him. I would also fear my mother more than I would fear me. But he apparently fears you more than either of us. At this moment, his wits are likely staining his short linens. But I cannot blame him for that, either."

"Because you are afraid of me?"

"I am not." Her quiet answer released a band of tension within his chest, and his heart seemed to beat more easily. "I expect you will kill me for all that I have said today, but there are worse things than death."

Kael could not think of any. He had experienced many different kinds of suffering throughout his life, and he preferred all of them to death. Of course, he *much* preferred the deaths of those who had made him suffer—and that preference had made him a king.

If she married him, it would make her a queen. "Yet still you came here, believing I would kill you?"

"Believing you would soon die in battle—or that *I* would kill *you*." She shrugged. "Everything must be in balance. We must endure something we don't want in order to secure something we do."

Spoken like anyone born in Ivermere. Those spellcasters knew nothing of balance. Their magic was always a trade, but never an equal one. "What is it you want?"

"What you have."

His kingdoms. Kael grinned, for he could admire her ambition—and her manner of securing what she wanted. "And what must you endure? Me?"

"Yes."

He laughed. So the princess believed she would have to survive him. She would no doubt be happy to learn that he had no intention of killing her, no matter her intentions toward him.

Softly she added, "But I'm certain I will learn to tolerate your touch—and I will bear the pain of your bed. A year is not so very long to endure it."

His chest filling with hot molten lead, he fell silent and followed Minam until the chamberlain halted at the entrance to a softly lighted bedchamber.

"Begone," Kael told him.

After only a brief hesitation, the other man fled.

Striding into the chamber, Kael carried Princess Anja directly to her bed—where he dumped her onto the embroidered coverlet. She sprawled onto her back in a tumble of silken limbs and white hair, blinking up at him in confusion and no small measure of uncertainty.

"Do not fear I'll join you," he told her harshly. "The only thing you have to endure is the journey back to Ivermere—where you will remain. I won't take you as my bride."

Her cheeks paled. "But you sent for—"

"I sent for no one. Though you are welcome to wed the

overzealous chamberlain who did." If Kael did not kill Minam for bringing this woman here. For giving Kael a glimpse of everything he wished to have. But unlike Anja, he would not endure something he didn't want to gain something he did. He would not endure mere tolerance.

Folding her arms over her stomach, she whispered, "You will not have me?"

"I will not."

She stared up at him, her dark gaze not seeming so bold now, but lost and uncertain. Abruptly she turned her head, hiding her face in a curtain of white hair. In a thick voice, she asked, "You vowed to help me crush the spider. Will you still do that?"

"I will." Whatever she believed, the Conqueror's word *did* mean something. "Rest for the remainder of this day. Tomorrow we leave at first light."

And he already cursed every moment that she would be in his sight. For the princess's magic had begun to work on his heart the moment he'd set eyes upon her—and he might be well and truly fucked before they reached Ivermere.

But not in the manner he wished to be.

2

ANJA THE REJECTED

Grimhold

BY ANJA'S RECKONING, SHE HAD slept for twenty days—and despite the lingering effects of the kissing potion, she did not sleep again that night.

Instead she cursed the day that the Conqueror's chamberlain had sent his letter, seeking a bride for his king. She cursed the day she'd read it and believed she could make a place for herself here. She cursed the day she'd seen the spider and every day that no one had believed that it was there. She cursed the day her mother had slipped the kissing potion into her drink. She cursed the day she'd arrived in Grimhold and revealed all of her plans to the one man who shouldn't have heard them.

But she cursed *this* day most of all.

As ordered, she was ready by first light—dressed to ride, as the Conqueror had sent word to her chambers that they would travel by horseback, not by carriage as she had arrived. The return home would only take fifteen days.

Only fifteen days until all of Ivermere knew that she had been rejected. No one at home would be surprised. The only surprise her father and mother had shown when she'd announced her intention to marry Kael the Conqueror was that she believed he might have her. That *anyone* would have her. Even a man so desperate for a bride that he'd had to send for one.

They wouldn't be surprised to discover they'd been right. Nor would they be surprised to learn that it was Anja's unguarded mouth that had ruined everything.

The only surprise, truly, was that she was still alive. Never had Anja dreamed that the moment she arrived, that she would tell Kael of her intentions. So she had expected the cool reception from the ladies who'd attended her the previous evening—after all, she had just threatened to assassinate their king—yet it had been some hours before she'd understood from their tightly worded replies that they all believed that *Anja* had changed her mind upon meeting him.

She did not know if Kael had told them that was what had happened in the sitting chamber, or if that was what they assumed. But it must be the reason she had not been dragged by her hair to an executioner's table.

That fear returned when, at dawn, she was escorted to the great hall, where a number of courtiers had gathered. To see her beheaded?

Upon the throne, Kael wore a thunderous expression as he spoke to the royal chamberlain. *You are more handsome than you should be*, she had told him last night, but she must have been blinded by the potion. For he was not handsome. That was a description better suited to courtiers who sculpted and shaped their features into perfect balance. But there was no balance to be found in Kael's appearance. Everything about him was too big, too hard, too volatile—as if a mountain had been chiseled down to its volcanic heart and shaped into a man.

Suddenly his ferocious blue eyes rose to meet hers. The chamber fell silent and accusing stares turned in her direction.

"Princess Anja!" His deep voice echoed through the large hall. Like a bolt released from a crossbow, he leapt from the throne and swiftly moved across the chamber, arrowing toward her. A sword was sheathed at his back. Did he always carry one, or was that blade meant for her?

Anja barely stopped herself from reaching for her own sword. She suspected her skill was nothing to his and that her attempt would do nothing but amuse him.

The fire in his blue gaze darkened as it slid down her form, taking in her heavy winter tunic, her fur-lined leggings, and her long coat of thick gray wolfskin. "You *can* ride a horse? I did not ask."

"I can." She rode every day…except for the past twenty. "The distance will be no hardship for me."

Her answer appeared to please him. The thunderous expression disappeared, but the guttural hardness of his voice didn't soften. Each word sounded as if it had been bitten off, but remained unswallowed. "We will leave shortly." He shot an irritated glance over his broad shoulder. "First there are a few matters for my attention."

"Of course," she murmured.

"Break your fast if you have not— You there." He pointed to a sleepy-eyed page who was not so sleepy-eyed after being singled out. "Show the princess to the dining hall. I will join you in a few moments."

Without waiting for an answer, he strode back to the throne. Never had she seen anyone move as he did, almost prowling as he walked, yet punctuated by bursts of speed that erupted with tension and force. At the dais, he sprang onto the marble platform and dropped into his golden throne, pounding his fist upon the table in front of him.

"Who is next?" he bellowed. "Hurry, fool! I have a quest to begin."

A quest. As if their journey was an adventure for him rather than an irritant caused by a bride he didn't want. He was so astonishingly different than anything she'd heard described. Oh, he was as huge as the rumors had claimed, and so strong that even his loose tunic could not conceal the sinewy bulge of his muscles. His powerful thighs looked as if they might rip the seams of his leather breeches with every movement. Everything about him was untamed and proud and seething against restraint.

Or bursting *through* restraint, when he slammed his seal upon a document and flung it away.

"Next!"

At the rate he was going through them, it would not give her much time to eat.

"Lead the way," she told the young page.

WHEN SHE RETURNED, IT SEEMED the number of officials who waited to see him had grown. Waiting near the doors, Anja listened to a commissioner ask for permission to send more soldiers to Lyngfen in hopes of catching the bandits that plagued the roads, until her attention was taken by a man in red silk hurrying to her side. Lord Minam, the royal chamberlain. Anja had liked the man upon first meeting him. Though he had nervous tendencies, he seemed kind—and she understood where those tendencies might have stemmed from. Geofry had been a monster—and *this* king…she truly did not know what to think of him. Her every expectation had been shattered.

Simply because he had spared her life.

"Your highness," Minam said as he reached her side. "Our king asks me to assure you that it will only be a moment before you and he begin the journey to Ivermere."

Judging by the number of officials, it would be longer than a moment. But there was no response to give except— "That is very kind of him."

A smile wreathed his face. "Yes! Not many see that he is. I am very glad you do."

And *she* was glad she had not been executed. Carefully Anja said, "Did he speak of what I told him?"

The man's smile faded. "Only that you decided not to wed him, after all."

"Oh."

Confusion swirled. He had lied to them, and said he had been the one rejected. Why?

With lowered voice, the chamberlain said, "Forgive me, your highness—but I hope that on this journey you will take time to reconsider."

I won't take you as my bride.

Her throat ached. "I do not think a change is likely."

Disappointment filled the man's face. "It is true that he is coarse, and loud, and always springing up and moving about as if hunting for something to kill. But he feels great responsibility to those under his protection. No doubt you heard of the bloodied path of destruction he laid through the four kingdoms as he rid our lands of Geofry's warlords, but those tales of slaughter do not fully describe him. Why…" Suddenly his expression brightened and he waved a serving girl over. "Only yesterday he saved this girl's life."

Still trying to find a bride for his king. Despite herself, Anja was charmed by the attempt. This chamberlain so clearly admired his ruler and cared about his happiness. "Did he?"

"He did. Tell her, Marna. Go on."

The girl peered up at her with wide, guileless eyes. "It's true, princess! I would have run past a ward. But he stopped me! I might have been ripped to shreds by your magic."

Anja could not halt her smile. "Or ended up with hair as white as mine."

White beyond a crone's white, and more like the white of a ghost—or so Anja had been told. She quite liked it. She was one of the few who did.

Obviously the girl was not part of that small number. Her eyes widened with horror. "Indeed, princess!"

Anja had great sympathy for the girl's fear, but Marna had nothing to fear from her. "Soon I will be gone, but you should always heed the wards. They are there for good reason."

The girl's smile widened—and was the only genuine smile turned Anja's way. Strange that those resentful stares were not because of what she'd done in truth, but because they believed she'd rejected their king.

Lord Minam had not given up. "If you delayed your journey, you might come to know him better. Is this spider so dangerous?"

"I believe it is."

"Your mother is a great spellcaster, as is your father."

"Yes." So Anja didn't know why they were blind to the threat. "But it is my duty as their daughter to protect them."

Even if they didn't want her protection.

"Could you not delay until after the Midwinter celebration? It is only two weeks hence."

Will you not have me?

I will not.

Thickly she answered, "I think not, my lord."

He heaved a great sigh. "I pray then that you will come to see him as I do. He is more patient and even-tempered than you would—"

"*Enough!*" The shout echoed through the room. The table in front of the throne upended, sending scrolls aloft like flies from a corpse. "There is nothing here that cannot wait until my return. Begone, all of you! Or stay. I don't care what you do."

"And he is very amicable," finished the chamberlain weakly.

Kael stalked toward them. As he crossed the hall attendants ran beside him, handing him a sleeveless chainmail hauberk that he dragged over his head, a quilted tunic to go over the armor, and a black fur cloak to fasten around his shoulders. Next they began to give him weapons, which he sheathed at his back, belt, and boots. By the time he reached her, the king was prepared for both battle and the weather. "Are you ready, Princess?"

"I am."

He held out one massive hand, and after a moment she realized he meant to carry the satchel containing the items she was bringing along. The leather sack was designed to be slung over her shoulder, but she had taken it and her coat off while waiting. "Oh, no. Thank you, but I—"

Without heeding her protest, he snatched it up. To Minam he said, "If you have anything more for me, you have until we reach the courtyard to say it."

Minam had much more, it seemed. His quick steps matched the Conqueror's long pace. "I beg you to reconsider your decision to travel unaccompanied—"

"I will not."

"If not courtiers, at least soldiers."

Anja looked at Kael in surprise. No one to accompany them?

Her breath caught as the brightness of his blue eyes turned on her. Humor curved his firm lips. "Can a sorceress as powerful as an Ivermeren princess not protect me?"

She tore her gaze away from his eyes, his smile. "I think you need no protection."

"You might be the only one a danger to me." Humor still laced his voice but it was harder now. A warning. "She will bind my heart and ensorcel my soul, Minam."

That mockery sliced her open like a blade, for he had made it very clear she could do nothing of the sort. But there was nothing she could say in response.

He turned to the chamberlain. "Or do you insist upon an escort for her sake? Do you think I cannot protect her?"

The chamberlain did not dare answer that.

Clapping his hand over the smaller man's shoulder, Kael reassured him, "We will have no reason to stray from the King's Road to the Scalewood passage, so if you have need of me, we will be easy to find. The princess has said the threat is urgent, so we must go quickly—and the more who accompany us, the slower we travel. The trunks full of the belongings she brought will follow in a caravan. Send soldiers with them, and if we meet any trouble, they would not be far behind."

"Yes, my liege." Minam sounded resigned. "But will you not delay another hour? We expect the envoy from Winhelm to arrive, with answers to our query regarding the soldiers who are amassing near the southern pass."

Kael's face became grim. "The message I have for King Frewin does not need to come from me. Tell him that if their army is not dispersed by spring, I will soon be the ruler of five kingdoms."

"Yes, my king," the chamberlain said unhappily.

They emerged from a large stone hall into a courtyard. The air was sharp and cold, the sun bright. At the center of the yard stood two horses—one a giant nightmare of a steed, and the other its prancing, snorting twin.

Kael saw her expression and grinned. "They are as kittens."

"I would not call you a liar to your face."

Laughing, he lifted her astride the nightmare before she could protest. "They are both strong enough to carry me."

"That is sensible." A palfrey would tire under the burden of his giant frame, and on such a journey, they could not be certain one of the horses wouldn't be injured or fall lame. Finding another horse for Anja would be easy. Not so for him.

He held up her satchel. "Shall I tie this to the saddle or do you wish to carry it?"

"I'll carry it." Anja slung the strap over her shoulder and across her breasts, then adjusted her sword sheathed at her back so that the satchel wouldn't interfere with drawing her weapon.

Kael looked her over, then nodded before leaping up into his saddle.

"You have my seal," Kael said to Minam. "Use it well. But do not send for more brides."

The chamberlain flushed. "Yes, my king."

The Conqueror swung his horse around. Anja nudged hers forward, and they started off at a brisk pace—too brisk for conversation. Yet she had little to say, anyway. All the amusement she'd felt earlier had fled, and a sick knot lodged in her chest as they began this trek home. If not for the urgent reason to return to Ivermere, she would have slipped out of the fortress in the night and ridden south, left this humiliation behind, until she reached a land with no expectations of her, and there was no shame in being herself.

Then they passed through the outer gate, and her breath was taken away. For she had *known* that the mountain fortress in Grimhold was a truly astonishing feat, but she had been sleeping through their arrival. Never had she seen anything so imposing—or so beautiful. Carved from the mountain itself, it soared upwards in heaven-piercing spires, and spread outward, overlooking a deep chasm crossed by a wide stone bridge.

They slowed the horses to a walk as they approached the bridge, allowing her the opportunity to say, "The stronghold is so very impressive. All the more so because no magic made it."

Kael cast a glance over his shoulder at the fortress. A grunt was his response before he looked forward again. "With enough slaves, a king needs no magic. He needs instead a sword stabbed through his head."

She could not argue with that. Looking over the side of the bridge to the chasm below dizzied her, so she studied him as they rode forward. He seemed so eager to leave—yet was his kingdom under threat of war? Never had she seen so many demands upon a king's time, except when there was a looming danger. Yet surely he would not abandon his fortress for a month if there was?

"Do you truly intend to conquer Winhelm?"

His mouth tightened. "Only if Frewin leaves me no choice."

"By sending his army over the pass?"

"Yes."

"What argument does he have with you?"

"None that I have started. He fears I will not be satisfied with four kingdoms and intends to stop me before I can take his."

Given all that she had heard of Kael, she would have believed the same as Frewin. Yet now she was not so certain. "*Are* you satisfied with four?"

"I have not time enough in a day for five." With a suggestive arch of his brow, he looked to her again. "You wished to have your own kingdom. Shall we ride in that direction instead? You can conquer it with your magics and I will assist with my sword."

She smiled despite the hurt in her heart. She *would* like to ride south, and rule her own kingdom. Yet it was impossible. She tried to keep that pain out of her voice as she said, "I have heard their king has a sorcerer of his own."

"One so unskilled that he cannot even spy on me and see that I have no intention of invading their lands. He will be easily defeated."

She eyed him, trying to decide if he was jesting, or genuinely offering to help her conquer Winhelm. But it didn't matter. With a sigh, she said, "We must ride north."

He regarded her with curious amusement. "Is there truly a spider in her bedchamber, or was the potion giving you waking dreams?"

"There is truly a spider. But you are free to believe everything else I said was a potion dream."

His mouth hardened, the humor leaving his face. "I wish I could believe that."

So he would not forget her threats. Though he must not take them seriously if he meant to travel with her alone. Even last night, when she'd stood with a sword in her hand, he had not taken them seriously. Instead he had laughed when she had spoken of killing him.

There was no reason to kill him now. She would gain nothing. And she was no longer certain Kael was the man he was rumored to be—a monster who had deserved such killing.

Silence fell between them again.

A city lay at the opposite end of the bridge, the stone buildings appearing almost as old as the fortress. Either Kael did not often ride through the city or he did not often ride alone, for he received astonished looks at every turn. Many people simply stopped and stared, others turned to run—though not in fear, because those who fled returned with others at their side to silently watch him pass.

And then follow him silently through the streets. It was the strangest royal procession that Anja had ever taken part in.

Abruptly it ended, as Kael reined his horse to a stop, frowning at something ahead. He looked to a woman standing at entrance of a home, holding her daughter's hand. The young girl gaped up at them.

"What is happening there?"

The woman darted a glance at the square farther down the street, where a handful of people stood milling about a stone platform. "A sentencing today, your majesty. There were two found guilty this week."

Unexpectedly Kael dismounted, then looked up at Anja. "I will only delay a moment."

"Yes," she said dryly. "I have seen how short your moments are."

A faint smile crossed his mouth, and a moment later he was at her mare's side to help her down though she did not need the assistance. He asked the woman to look after their mounts and received tearfully happy reassurances that their horses would be cared for as she would her own children.

Such a strange man he was. Anja felt like one of the crowd following him, though not with the same awe that they showed, but sheer curiosity. A sentencing was a common occurrence, so it was strange that he would stop now to watch—especially after tossing a table and abandoning a room full of officials who had delayed his journey.

A magistrate in black robes sat beneath an awning, scrolls spread out on a table in front of him. Those being sentenced had already been found guilty; now they would hear the punishment that the magistrate had chosen. A woman in chains stood before him, but there was not a word said as Kael approached. He joined the small circle of observers—though that circle almost immediately grew to overfill the square, bodies packed close, except that an arm's length of empty space remained around Kael and Anja. The magistrate stood, looking out over the crowd, clearly overwhelmed and uncertain.

"My king," the man said unsteadily. "May I help you?"

"I am here to observe," he told the magistrate. "Continue."

"Of course, my liege," he said, sitting again. Nervously he shuffled papers, cleared his throat and began, "Shalen of Stonebrook, you have been found guilty of…" The magistrate hesitated, stumbling uneasily again before continuing, "of the crimes you committed, I sentence you to a silencing, wherein your tongue will be cut from your—"

"What was the crime?" Kael demanded.

"Crimes of slander, your majesty."

"She is to lose her tongue for that? What did she say?"

"I— That is, she—" The official mopped his sweating brow. "I do not wish to repeat them."

"But you *will* repeat them."

With shaking hands, the older man lifted the scroll and read, "For speaking slanderous words against the king, including calling him a violent, foul murderer; a barbaric, foreign usurper undeserving of the throne; and a rapist, I sentence you to—"

"You will sentence her for this?" Kael shook his head. "All but one of those are true."

"Shall I sentence her for the one that is a lie?" The magistrate hesitated. "Which is untrue?"

"I have never forced a woman," Kael said.

"But the rest are also monstrous accusations—"

Kael gave a harsh, short laugh. "And I have done monstrous things. After I broke the chains that held me in the mines, I fought my way into Qul Wrac's great hall. His magics shattered my hammer, so I ripped his jaw away before he could chant more spells. That was the moment he lost, but still my rage was such that I ripped out his tongue and used his own jawbone to rip him from gut to gullet. When I was finished, he lay in pieces around my bare feet and his blood painted every inch of my skin. Tell me, am I a violent murderer? Say truth."

Anja stared at him in horror. She had known what that slaver's fate had been. But never had such a picture been painted of it.

So she *had* heard the truth of him. Perhaps not the worst of it.

Stubbornly the magistrate said, "If I must say you are a murderer, then I will also say he deserved that bloody death, my king."

"You would say that of him, but not of me?" He gestured to the woman awaiting her sentence. "She has most of it right. Only the details are amiss, and she is hardly to blame for mistaking them. Will you sentence her for repeating what she has heard? I have been called the Raviner."

The magistrate squirmed. "That does not only mean that you have forced women. It also means your hunger is unceasing. That could be hunger for destruction or violence, not only for women."

Kael looked to Anja. "What did you take it for?"

She might as well be truthful; she had admitted to worse the past night. "I thought you ravished women against their will."

He appeared unsurprised by that confession. "And what did Shalen of Stonebrook think?"

To the guard, the magistrate said, "Allow her to speak."

The woman turned angry eyes upon Kael. "It means exactly what he has done. Any man with such violence in him, any man who needs such power—he will take it any way he can. That is a man who will force a woman."

The tension in the crowd swelled, with shouts rising in anger against the woman's words. Until Kael held up his hand. He looked to the magistrate again. "I have known too many men of whom that is true. I think she has also known such men and I cannot blame her for assuming that what is true of them is also true of me. Give her a full pardon and strike the law from the books. A citizen may say whatever she likes about the king."

Reeling with surprise, Anja stared at his profile, trying to reconcile that generous decision with the unyielding power standing before her. Around them, murmurs of disbelief and uncertainty joined the crackling shuffle of parchment as the magistrate rifled through his scrolls.

"That particular law does not only concern the king. Do you give all citizens leave to make monstrous claims about another's character?"

"If they say truth, they can say whatever they like. But if they speak ill, and are not certain whether it is true—or if they know it *not* to be true—they ought to be more careful with their words, for others might be harmed by them."

"And if someone is harmed by a lie?"

"That is a matter for the magistrates." He looked to the guards. "Release her now and provide protection for her until she reaches her home."

They hurriedly obeyed, opening the woman's chains—who turned and spat in Kael's direction before stalking out of the courtyard.

Anja looked to Kael, expecting him to respond to that insult, but he merely said to the magistrate, "Who is next?"

"Only one more, my king." He mopped his brow again while a short, thin man with soft eyes and fidgeting fingers was led out before the platform. The prisoner's hands twisted together as the magistrate announced his name, then read out the sentence. "For the crimes of thievery and murder, you have been found guilty, and I have considered both your attempt to undo what was done, as well as your refusal to show remorse or accept responsibility for your actions. Therefore I sentence you to—"

The prisoner didn't wait to hear what it was. "I wish to petition the king!"

"That is your right," the magistrate said. "The next Petition Day is—"

"Now," Kael interrupted. "I will hear your petition. Are you guilty?"

"I'll admit to the theft, and that I stole a coin because I was hungry. But I don't admit to killing anyone."

His face impassive, the magistrate offered, "There were witnesses who saw the stabbing, my king. Should I call for them?"

"I confess to using my blade, but it was not murder." Arguing earnestly, he continued, "His death wasn't my fault."

Anja frowned. "If you stabbed him, how can that be?"

A murmuring came from the crowd and all eyes turned to her as Kael spoke, "This is Princess Anja of Ivermere. Treat a question from her as if it were a question from me."

"Ivermere!" The thief's face lit. "You will surely agree that the fault was not mine, Princess. For we were at the Crowing Cock, you see? Mere steps from the healer's square. And I didn't mean to hurt him so bad, truly I didn't. But I lifted his coin, and he came after me, and I was in fear of my life. But once I got my knife into him, it was too deep, so I offered to carry him to the healer. And—"

"Your majesty, your highness," the magistrate interjected, "I am compelled to add that the prisoner only offered to carry him to the healer after he was confronted by witnesses to the stabbing. They stated that, prior to his offer to help, he attempted to run out of the tavern."

And would have left the man to die. But if the thief stayed, why *had* the man died? "Why was he not saved if the healer's square was so near?"

"He refused the healing," the prisoner claimed. "He said he was an abjurer."

Anja blinked in surprise and looked to the magistrate. "Truly?"

The older man nodded. "Witnesses confirmed his statement."

An abjurer. Anja had heard of those who refused to use magic of any sort, because the scale of the world must remain in balance—and so for every healing, there was a wounding. But it was not always equal. Sometimes the injury was small. Sometimes it was many times worse. It always changed in the scaling—and it always sought something living, which was why healers allowed only the person who needed help behind their wards, and kept cages of mice and insects for the magic to act upon. She had heard of people who refused to use magic for small injuries. But *never* had she heard of abjuring in such a case as mortal wounds.

"Truly." The thief nodded solemnly, his soft eyes gently imploring. "It was my knife that cut him, but he'd have lived. Except for that choice. He *chose* to die because he feared the scaling would kill another living thing, even if it was only one of the healer's mice. But the scaling might have done no more than pinch the mouse's belly."

Anja shook her head. Perhaps the man had refused the healing, but the fault here was clear. "That is not true. Only one choice here killed him, and that was when you chose to stab him."

"I could not know he was an abjurer, and we were so near to the healer's square. I believed no harm would be done."

She was unmoved by that argument. "Then it is your fault for not asking him about his beliefs before you stuck him with your blade."

Seeing she would not be the ally he'd hoped for, the prisoner turned his soft eyes toward the king and met the grave hardness of Kael's features.

His voice as rough and sharp-edged as gravel, Kael said, "You ought to withdraw your petition. Whatever the magistrate's sentence is, it is likely more lenient than mine."

"But it was not my fault!"

"No?" With a hard smile, Kael drew his sword. "When I sliced Eathe of Vale open, he held in his guts as he fled. He made it almost four hundred paces before dropping dead. How far away is the healer's square?"

"Only fifty paces, my king," the magistrate answered.

"Tell me," Kael asked the thief, "whose fault is your death if you cannot reach the healer's square after I open you up?"

Desperate, he tried again. "That is not the same. His refusal—"

"Was a refusal he would not have had to make if you hadn't stuck him with a blade!" Kael roared. "It was your knife that killed him. If you disagree, we will test how far you can run—and make no mistake, *I* will have killed you. Do you wish to receive my sentence?"

The thief wildly shook his head.

Kael looked to the magistrate. "I leave you to it."

Taking Anja's hand, he pulled her with him—perhaps so she would not be lost as he pushed his way through the crowd. Except there was no pushing. From the square to the street where their horses stood waiting, the crowd fell back at his approach. Fearing the sword he still carried—or the thunder on his face.

A young girl with curly brown hair darted out into

the street and into his path, bringing them to an abrupt halt. Anja judged her only three or four years of age.

"Bela!" A woman rushed out after her, only to freeze at the sight of the king towering over her daughter, sword in his hand. A cry broke from her lips, terror paling her face.

Smiling up at him, her eyes bright, the child held up a small, dried flower, with petals so brown that Anja barely recognized it as a daisy.

Kael looked down at her. "What is this?"

"He hates flowers," came a hiss from the crowd. "He forbade them in the fortress."

Moaning in abject fear, the mother pressed forward and lifted her hand beseechingly. "My king, please forgive her."

"What is to be forgiven?" Sheathing his sword, he knelt. "You are only showing this to me, young one, or giving it to me?"

"Giving." She thrust the flower at him. "You will be happy?"

She pointed to his frowning mouth, which slowly curved upward.

"Indeed it does." With his huge, battle-scarred hand, Kael carefully lifted the dried daisy from her tiny fingers. "Now be kind to your mama, little one, and run back to her arms. And always remember she braved the Raviner himself to keep you safe."

The girl skipped back to her tearful mother. Continuing down the cobblestone street, Anja watched him in open astonishment until they reached the horses. There he glanced down at the flower—clearly at a loss, for he could not throw it away, nor was it feasible to continue clutching the stem while he rode, and stowing it in a satchel would destroy the fragile dried petals.

Biting her lip against a smile, Anja offered, "Let me help you."

Gladly he gave the flower over, then frowned when she crooked her finger.

"Bend your head."

He did, and his eyes seemed like blue fire, intense on hers and very close as she tucked the stem into a link of chain mail at his throat, the backs of her fingers brushing warm skin. "It will not survive long, but it will remain long enough for her to see you wear it—and forever in her memory."

"Her mother's, too," he said wryly.

With a smile of agreement, Anja indicated that he could straighten again. "I have also just braved the Raviner," she said softly. "Will you be kind to me?"

Gruffly he answered, "Magic is your domain, not mine."

Her lips seemed to freeze into their smile. "A spell cannot make anyone kind."

Just as it could not make anyone fall in love. Or make them hate.

His puzzled frown made her realize she had mistaken his meaning. But she could barely fathom his when he said, "Of course it cannot. Kindness is of the purest magic. It cannot be corrupted by a spellcaster's chantings."

She did not know which part of his statement to answer first. Spellcasting was not a corruption. It created beauty, and gave strength, and restored health. But she began with the most absurd part. "Kindness is not magic."

Kael drew back from her. "Spoken as any Ivermeren sorceress would. You know only one sort of magic." Without warning he grasped her waist and effortlessly hefted her astride her horse, then turned toward his own. "But I wield no magic at all, and certainly not kindness. I am Kael the Pitiless."

The man who escorted her back to Ivermere, though she had threatened to kill him? The man who had pardoned a woman, though every other king Anja knew would have punished her? "Pitiless?" she echoed. "That is not what I have seen."

Dismissing that with a short, harsh laugh, Kael swung into the saddle and gathered up his reins. "Then I am certain I will show you before we journey much longer."

3

KAEL THE PITILESS

Grimhold

THOUGH THEIR LEAVING HAD BEEN delayed, the day's ride upon the King's Road took them halfway across Grimhold. As the main thoroughfare that connected the kingdoms, the road wound past so many villages and inns that travelers needed to carry few supplies. That day, they rode until full dark. Had he been alone, Kael would have continued on, but he could not as closely watch Anja and see how she fared after darkness fell.

She had been quiet since leaving the city near the stronghold. Kael did not know if it was the lingering effects of the potion and of almost three weeks of inactivity, or her own uncertainty. He had not mistaken her horror when he had described how he had killed Qul Wrac—and he had been deliberate in that description, so she knew there was no use in attacking him, if that was still her intention. He wasn't certain it was. He wasn't certain what she thought about anything. He could make little sense of her. She had been horrified, then touched him and smiled at him.

Though she probably did the same: tried to make sense of him. He had seen her studying him throughout the day. Perhaps trying to fathom his thoughts.

He could have told her his thoughts didn't stray far from her hands. He could still feel the burn of her touch on his throat. The flower she'd placed there had crumbled hours before, but the brush of her fingers lingered on his skin.

So his two weeks of torment had begun. And it would only worsen while they slept.

The swiftness with which Kael was accommodated at the public house ought not to have surprised him, yet still it did. In years past, they would have let him in—too fearful not to—but hoped he would remain in the corner, quietly have his supper, and move on without taking a room.

Here he secured two bedchambers and saw the inn-keeper's confusion that there were not any attendants, particularly as the princess was with him. She had insisted on attending to herself, and had given him a dour look when he'd reminded her to add wards to the walls before using her magic to fix her hair or unlace her tunic.

Sleep was nowhere near his mind when her yawn sent her from their dining table to bed. Unwilling to leave her unprotected, however, he went up the stairs and into the adjoining room, where he would be near her if any threat arose.

Though the tavern had been lively while they dined, almost immediately everything within the public house quieted. From below came a clattering, followed by a hissed, "Silence! The king sleeps!"

The king didn't sleep. The king fisted his cock and remembered the way Anja's nightgown had revealed her form, and her firm grip upon her sword. He pumped his aching shaft while in his mind he ripped the silk down the length of her body, baring her fully to his sight. The king groaned and stroked harder when the faint sound of a splash came from the next chamber, because he knew she was bathing, and that her flesh would be clean and wet and fresh, ripe enough to eat. Had that wetness been for him, he would have parted her thighs and feasted for the rest of his life.

Instead the king allowed himself to imagine plunging into her hot cunt, of burying his fingers in her white hair as he fucked deep. He pictured her pleasure as she writhed beneath him, and his mind echoed with her soft cries when his seed spurted into his hand.

Leisurely he washed it away, listening to the sounds from the next room, waiting for the creak of the bed.

Before long, the sound came. She was ready to sleep, then.

And with his body satisfied, Kael was ready as well.

Taking his sword, wearing only his breeches and unlaced tunic, he stopped at the door to her room. "I would enter, Princess."

There was a rustle of cloth and the pad of bare feet. The sound of the latch raising.

A single lamp burned inside the chamber, offering enough light to see her by and casting an orange glow over white hair plaited into a braid that hung over her shoulder. She had put on her long coat as a robe over her heavy winter tunic, which she must have decided to sleep in. Beside her bed leaned her sword, within easy reach. Over the back of a chair draped her leggings.

He had not realized she'd worn leather stockings of that design—not tied at the waist, as his breeches were, but each one drawn up the length of her legs and secured with ties at the tops of her thighs.

His sated cock was already stirring again. But no matter how he turned the matter over in his mind, he saw no option but one.

He strode inside. "We will sleep in the same chamber."

Her gaze searched his face. "You fear attack?"

"From you or from my people?"

Her cheeks flushed.

"I do not fear your magics," he said. "Your sword while I sleep is another matter."

"You can latch your door—"

"A lock is nothing to a child, let alone a sorceress." He moved her sword from the bedside, placing it near the hearth, then picked up the two leather straps she used to secure her leggings.

He held out one. "Get into the bed and tie this strap around your ankles."

Her lips parted and she stared at him in disbelief. But only a moment passed before she realized, "You are serious."

"I am. Last eve you spoke of your intentions to kill me. I would be a fool to sleep without tying you."

Her gaze slid away from his. Though shaking her head, she obediently slipped off her coat and scrambled into her bed, winding the strap around her ankles. Mouth tightly pursed, she held out her wrists.

Swiftly he bound her arms together. "Move over."

Again she gaped at him. "You intend to share my bed?"

"These ties are nothing for a conjurer to loosen. If I left you here alone, you could free yourself and slice open my throat without ever waking me." And he was not that foolish. "Next to you, I would awaken if you move. I have no intention of taking more. I have no interest having you."

No interest in a woman who shook in fear and would not welcome his touch.

"So you have said." The lilting cadence of her voice had flattened, and anger burned in her cheeks. "I do not welcome your company."

"In my place, what would you do?"

"I assumed you'd kill me by now." She sighed. "Perhaps

sharing a bed is not so terrible in comparison."

Perhaps not for her. When she scooted over and turned onto her side, Kael snuffed the lamp and got beneath the covers. Though she stiffened in protest, he pulled her back against his chest, draped his arm around her waist, and pushed his thigh between hers, just above her knees. Now she could not possibly move without his knowing.

Her body rigid with tension, she shook helplessly against him.

"Be at ease," he commanded.

"I will try," she whispered. After a moment, she added softly, "You did not fully escape being a king this day."

Because when they had arrived at the public house, slowly and with gathering courage, some of the villagers had approached him with their concerns. But speaking with them had not been tedious. It had not been rituals and reports but the lives of his people. "I do not seek to escape my duty."

"I did not think you meant to escape your duty. Only the endless demands upon you."

"They are the same." But at least the number of reports he'd listened to upon his throne had prepared him to answer many of the questions they'd had. "And that is what a king does."

He felt her nod, and slowly she relaxed against him, her body pressing more fully against his. Sleepily she said, "Will you remove your sword from between us?"

Gritting his teeth, he ground out, "I cannot."

"I do not wish to impale myself if I turn in my sleep."

A choked laugh escaped him. "The only flesh this sword would pierce is between your thighs. But unless those thighs and your mouth first open in invitation, you have no fear of that."

She went utterly still again as his meaning sank in. Not shaking, but stiff against him.

She would sleep soon enough. Kael closed his eyes and willed his own body to drowse.

Wakefulness found him again at a tug against his arm. Anja. Not trying to get away, only moving her bound arms as if to find a more comfortable position. Then she did it again. Then gave her head a little shake, tickling his throat with her hair, and every single fidgeting movement rubbed her ass in tiny increments against his cock, driving him to madness.

"Be still," he said gruffly.

"I have an itch on my cheek," she whispered back. "I don't know if it's my hair or if there's something on me, and I can't use my hands to get it off."

Lifting his head, in the dim light he saw the many-legged shadow against her fair skin. On a sharp breath, he blew it from her cheek and rested his head against the pillow again.

"It was only a brown crawler," he said. "It's gone now."

He'd thought to reassure her, but that didn't. Wildly she swiped at her face, her hair. "A crawler?"

"I blew it across the bed."

Immediately she shoved back against him with such force that he almost tumbled over the edge. "Where is it?"

"If you do not use your magics, you have no reason to fear it."

"I have reason to fear it will bite me!"

That sort of crawler didn't even have fangs. "It is a harmless—"

"I just felt it!" With her bound hands, she slapped at the covers, then at her legs. "I think it's on me. I *feel* it on me."

He couldn't bear the panic in her voice. "Hold still." As she lay panting and trembling, he sat up and examined the bedcovers. Against the white linens, it was easy to spot the insect.

He slipped his hand beneath the crawler and carried it to the window, nudging it from his palm with his forefinger before closing the shutter again.

Lying on her back, a wide-eyed Anja stared at him as he crossed the chamber toward the bed. "You didn't kill it?"

Why would he? "It did us no harm, and I'm not hungry. Slide over again."

Though Anja scooted over, instead of turning onto her side, she continued watching him. He felt her gaze through the dark as he slid beneath the covers, and as he pulled her close again. "Sleep now," he commanded.

She pillowed her head on his biceps. Several minutes passed before she softened against him. Then she found her sleep.

He closed his eyes and found his own.

4

ANJA THE UNWANTED

Vale

ON THE FOURTH MORNING ANJA woke to the first snow of the season. Though it stopped falling before dawn and the sun rose, the air remained cold enough that the snow didn't melt as they set out upon the King's Road again. For miles, all around them stretched the fields of Vale, lying fallow for the winter and now blanketed in white.

She glanced over at Kael, and found him watching her intently. Always he seemed to either watch her intently or intently not watch her, but he was watching her now with narrowed eyes. Each time this morning, that look had been followed by his asking whether she was warm enough within her wolfskin coat.

But now there was different focus.

"I had thought your hair was white as snow. But now to compare, it is even whiter."

Her smile felt tight. "Like a ghost's?"

"No. Theirs is white, but it's a foul and unclean white."

Her lips parted in surprise. "You have seen a ghost?"

He nodded. "As a boy, in the Dead Lands. There is nothing of beauty in their hair. But yours is like winter."

"Thin, cold, hungry?"

He frowned. "Are you hungry?"

"Not at this moment."

"Are you cold?"

"No." She shook her head. "I did not mean my... I meant that winter often conjures thoughts of being alone outside in the cold."

"Your hair conjures thoughts of the fairest part of winter." He gestured to the snowcapped peaks in the distance. "Like the sun gleaming across the mountains."

She had never been called beautiful before. At home, she sometimes thought the trends of fashion and beauty were to look *unlike* her. No one wanted to resemble Ivermere's shame.

Touched by his words, she said, "I think you must be as summer, then."

Hot and vibrant with life—but not new life, as in spring, but fully formed and vital.

"I am winter, too. But a fat, hibernating bear, softened

in his den."

"You are soft?"

"Being a king has made me so."

She could not halt a peal of laughter. Never had she seen any person built as hard as he was. Even at rest, his muscles felt unyielding as stone, and awake they had as much give as a steel wall.

"If you are soft now, then before you were king, you must have been as…" She trailed off, at a loss. "If you are steel and stone now, what is harder than that?"

"I can think of a few things," was his dry reply. "One you feel each night."

Yet again she could not stop her laugh, though her face flamed, and though she could not bear his intent look now and averted her gaze from his.

Three nights had he lain behind her. If he had been as steel, then she had been the furnace at the making of it.

Though it had not been true the first night. That night, she had been tense and uncertain. Then he had saved a crawler. That was the moment when she'd realized he truly wasn't the man she had thought he was. After that, she hadn't felt nervous in his arms. She'd felt safe.

But each night, with fear gone, she'd also thought about offering the invitation he'd spoken of. It could do little harm to her if she was not a virgin; no one would have her anyway.

But Kael had already said he would not, either. And he must have plenty of willing women in his bed. Surely the stronghold had no shortage of them.

She could not bear to think of those women waiting for his return. And she would try not to think about how it felt to lie against him with her body afire. She would *not* be a dong-addled maiden, pining for a man who had already rejected her—and not even for the same reason everyone else had.

She could not blame him for that reason, though. He hadn't sent for a bride—and surely wouldn't accept one who announced she intended to kill him.

"Did your mother bed a man from Glacian?"

Startled, she looked to him. "Why would you suggest such a thing?"

He eyed her mouth, then her hair again. "Everyone in Ivermere has dark hair. But in the far north, there are peoples with hair almost as pale as yours."

"Oh. No." Embarrassment heated her face. "I was hiding from my nursemaid, and had concealed myself in my mother's quarters. She cast a spell to redden her lips and this was the scaling."

He frowned. "What of your natural wards?"

Because everyone who wielded magic could be affected by a spell, but they were resistant to the scaling. Avoiding his eyes, she shrugged. "My mother is a powerful sorceress."

"And you are her daughter, and your father's daughter. Your power would be theirs combined."

"No young girl is more powerful than a queen," she said. "And I ought to have known better than to be in her chambers. Her magic is so strong that there are wards on every wall to keep it from spilling out."

Just as walls and shutters kept light from escaping a closed room.

His mouth twisted. "It spills over into Scalewood. All the corrupted magic in Ivermere does. That is why monsters roam that forest."

She shook her head. He had it backward. "My people developed their magic to protect themselves from the monsters in Scalewood."

"Is that what is said in Ivermere?" He narrowed his eyes. "Your sort of magic is deliberate. Spells must be cast. Do you think the trees and deer were chanting spells and corrupting their own home?"

Perhaps he was right. But it was long ago and no one could know. "Even if that is true, you cannot deny that terrible magic lies within the forest now."

"So the magic of Scalewood spills back into Ivermere, and each generation is more powerful than before, and the forest more dangerous. Is that not true?"

"It is said," she agreed. Everything had to be in balance, so the civilized, purposeful magic scaled into something wild and chaotic. And the wild and chaotic magic of Scalewood scaled back.

"The Dead Lands used to be a green, bountiful realm. More fertile and abundant than Vale." He indicated the land around them.

"As Ivermere is," she said.

He nodded. "And there were sorcerers so powerful, even death was not an end. Then one spell scaled so mightily, there was a great Reckoning, and the realm and its peoples were all but destroyed."

She had heard that story before, but not with the gravity that he told it. "I thought the Reckoning was only a legend? A warning to spellcasters not to try to raise the dead."

"It is truth. In Ivermere, they might comfort themselves by calling it only legend." He shrugged. "But in time, Ivermere and Scalewood will be as the Dead Lands."

A horrifying thought, yet although he had been born in the Dead Lands, he only shrugged to think about it happening again? Or perhaps he believed it was what they deserved? He had no care for Ivermere.

"Do you dislike magic?" Another thought occurred to her. "You have called it corrupt. Are you an abjurer?"

She could hardly fathom that anyone was, whether they could cast spells or not. Not when magic did so much good and helped so many. But it was true that the scaling did seek out a balance. So often, that was harmless. But there was reason why healers kept cages of mice within their wards—so that if the scaling was harmful, it would have a target not human.

"I'm not an abjurer." Kael seemed amused at the thought. "I mislike the spellcasters' use of magic. For it is not the scaling that is corrupted, but the use."

Healing was a corrupt use? "Would you not risk a

mouse to save a human life?"

"I would," was his immediate answer. "But I do not lie to myself as spellcasters do to comfort themselves. That sort of healing is rarely needed. More likely, a scrape would be healed. Most of a spellcaster's magic is nothing but impatience and laziness."

"Laziness?" She stared at him in amazement. "It requires years of study and constant mindfulness."

As her parents reminded her constantly.

"Healing can be done without magic, too. That requires true study—and patience, for healing naturally is never quick. It also harms no one. That is the spellcasters' lie, that there is little harm done, because it cannot be known how a spell will scale. I would not injure a mouse for a scrape—or to redden my lips."

That she could understand well. Even in Ivermere, there was argument about when it was appropriate to use magic. "Nor would I."

The arch of his eyebrow was faintly mocking. "So you learned a lesson from your hair? You are rare for an Ivermeren."

Rarer than he suspected. "I could not have failed to learn a lesson from it. My mother made certain I knew it was my own fault for walking into her chambers uninvited."

"Your fault?" He frowned. "How old were you?"

"Three years of age."

A foul oath spat from his tongue, followed by— "Only a shit-witted slopmouth would have done so."

A pang struck her chest even as a flush heated her cheeks. Being the daughter of a king and queen, never had she been called a slopmouth to her face—but it had likely been said many times behind her back. And she had been told that worthless swill fell from her lips when she spoke, which was the same. "I know. I was old enough to know better."

"You mistake me," he said grimly. "I was speaking of your mother for blaming you. Your mother was old enough to know better than to be so careless. What of the kissing potion? Will she blame you for that, as well?"

The flush rose to an embarrassed burn through her entire face. Anja could imagine what her mother would say—and her father. They would not see the irony that her mother had given Anja the potion to make certain she would marry Kael, yet it was the potion that had loosened her lips and made certain she would not. And they would be unsurprised that she had been felled by her unguarded tongue. Spellcasters believed nothing was more shameful or dangerous than uncareful words—and Anja had spoken many in her life. They would only say that it was more of the same, that there was justice and balance in being defeated by her own words, especially if she had simply stopped insisting that a spider was in her mother's bedchamber, if she had simply shut her mouth, the potion wouldn't have been necessary.

Perhaps they were right. And Anja did not know who to blame. She didn't know if blame mattered at all now.

Blaming would not change the past, or make Kael take her to wife. It would not change that she would be returned to Ivermere, even more unwanted than when she'd left.

But she couldn't bear to think of what her welcome home would be, and instead thought back to something else he'd said. "You speak of Ivermere's magic as corrupt magic."

"Because it is."

"But you claim kindness is pure magic?"

He smiled faintly. "Because it is."

"I have never heard of such a thing. I do not think anyone in Ivermere has."

He shrugged, unbothered by her doubt. "That does not make it untrue. What is magic but an unseen force that works change upon the world? That is what kindness does. I have not known much of it myself but I have seen its power many times."

She could only stare at him, something within her filling up as he spoke, but still unable to comprehend his words. Never had she heard anyone speak of kindness so matter-of-factly, as if this was a subject well known to him. Yet he'd said he'd not known it himself.

Perhaps that was *why* he knew of it. Everyone had heard of his past—how he had seen his clan and family slaughtered in the Dead Lands, then had been chained and sent across the Illwind Sea to the Four Kingdoms. There he was enslaved in the Blackworm mines until he'd broken his chains and killed the warlord who'd served

Geofry in that region.

Who would value kindness more than someone who'd been treated cruelly? Just as no one valued freedom more than someone who'd been enslaved.

Yet this was still not something she'd heard spoken of before in any of the nearby kingdoms. "Were you taught this in the Dead Lands?"

"It is well known there," he confirmed. "Kindness, courage, love—they are the most powerful of all magic."

How could he say that so indifferently? He rode along, telling her of powerful magics as if what he imparted was no great secret, though every one of her senses felt alive with the learning of it.

"You *truly* think they are magic?"

"I know it to be true." He looked to her, and she saw that he was not as indifferent as he appeared, for his eyes burned with absolute conviction. "I would sooner face a thousand soldiers strengthened by a sorcerer's spell than a dozen men filled with true courage or who are fighting for those they love."

That claim was not mere conjecture—for Anja had heard stories of how he *had* faced and defeated a thousand soldiers. He'd slaughtered his way toward Toatin Zan, and after slaying the sorcerer, the remaining army had fled.

But it was the manner of his speech that struck her so powerfully. Courage was always celebrated, and kindness and love were often spoken of as something good—yet also sweetly cloying, embarrassing to acknowledge with any real earnestness, and better suited to lessons learned in children's tales than to adult conversation. Certainly she'd never heard love spoken of with the reverence that Kael did, or heard the suggestion that it might win battles. And never had she been so drawn to an idea as she was drawn to the concept of magic as he described it…yet still she struggled to fully grasp the implications.

Kael had said he hadn't known much kindness and didn't wield that magic but… "Have you known love?" she asked.

His mouth firmed. For a long moment he only looked down the road ahead, then finally answered, "Not in many years. Not since my family was killed."

The undisguised grief in his reply tugged at her heart. But at least he had known *some* love. Anja had family living and could not say with truth whether she had ever known love at all.

"Then it was courage that helped you prevail against Toatin Zan." And against Geofry, and all of the others Kael had butchered in his campaign to free the four kingdoms.

"Courage, hate." His eyes narrowed slightly, as if he was peering into his memory. "Rage."

And each was its own magic? But it made sense. "So they each are balanced by the scale, too. Love and hate, fear and courage—"

"No. These magics have no scale."

"Of course they have a scale." Balance was the fundamental element of all magic. Letting her reins go, she lifted her hands, holding her right lower than her left. "If a spell is cast and magic heals on this side, then magic also injures on the opposite side." She brought her hands even. "The scale of the world must be in balance."

"No," he said.

Anja laughed. "No? Even the Conqueror cannot simply deny truth and make it so."

But he could draw his sword more swiftly than any swordmaster she'd seen. Yet even as she caught her breath and her gaze darted around the empty fields, searching for the threat, he merely tilted the shining steel this way and that.

"The world is not on a scale, just as this sword is not. It simply is. The corrupt magics create the scale—they force the world onto a fulcrum, and spells are the levers that move things within the world from one side to the other." Carefully he balanced the sword lengthwise on the horn of his saddle, the hilt toward her and the blade pointed toward the opposite side of the road. Lightly he pressed down on the hilt and the point rose higher into the air. "You say that when a healing spell is cast, magic of opposite weight is added to balance it."

"Yes," she said. "That is right."

He shook his head. "Corrupt magic creates nothing. It only moves what already exists from one place to another. You say it adds health, but it *steals* health from somewhere else, so that one side has more and the other less. If it was true balance, it would add health to both sides, not health on one and injury to the other." The handle tipped down farther. "But you say that a spell to redden lips adds color on one side, and adds a lack of color to the other side, so it would balance."

"Yes." Though she was not so certain now.

"No. Magic stole color from your hair and put it upon your mother's lips." He tipped the handle farther. "Corrupt magic does not find balance. Instead it forces everything that exists onto a scale and skews the world farther and farther out of balance with each spell, until—"

The sword slipped from the saddlehorn and dropped. Swiftly Kael leaned over, caught the weapon by the blade before it touched the ground, and sheathed it again. The lesson was finished—and Anja had never been a poor student.

"Until there is a Reckoning," she concluded softly.

His short nod confirmed her reply.

She shook her head—not in denial, but in disbelief. "My entire life, I have been surrounded by magic and studied it." Everyone in Ivermere did, no matter their natural talent. "Yet no one has ever explained magic as you have explained it."

"What reason would they?" His powerful shoulders lifted in another shrug. "It suits them to believe otherwise."

Anja could not see how. "How could it suit anyone?"

"Magic is a tool. But its use comes at a cost, and spell-casters are not the ones who pay it, because they have resistance to the scaling. Instead the price is paid by those who don't wield the corrupt magic."

"You speak as if you believe spellcasters care nothing of the effect of their magics on others."

A short laugh preceded his, "How are those who don't wield magic spoken of in Ivermere?"

Such shameful memories flooded Anja's mind that she could not even meet his eyes. "Not very well."

"The mines taught me what value a life has to someone who believes themselves superior. That value is not much."

Anja knew that was true, too. Her chest hurting, her throat thick, she watched the road unwind beneath her horse's hooves until she could easily speak again. "If what you say is true, then everyone can wield magic. Love and hate, kindness and—"

She broke off, because that wasn't quite correct. And even as she realized why it was not, a strange and wonderful giddiness rose through her that she could not contain. But it was Kael who spoke what she had only just understood.

"Everybody already *does*," he said gruffly, his blue gaze searing hers.

Tears filled her eyes. Quickly she tore her gaze from his, so overwhelmed by the wonder of it that she couldn't speak.

Into the quiet between them, he said, "Pure magics don't steal. They create, and add into the world something that wasn't there before—and the result is not the opposite. Kindness does not beget cruelty. Instead it begets hope and comfort."

Anja had not thought she could be any more astonished. Yet understanding slipped through her on another wave of wonder. She stared at him wide-eyed, and when he suddenly grinned at her, the giddiness that had been building within her burst into a laugh. "This is true!"

"It is."

"And love does not beget hate—but hate must beget that which is similar. Pain, fear."

Kael nodded. "Which in turn beget more of the same."

Sobering, she frowned thoughtfully. "I think one must be very careful with such magics, then—be careful not to let them loose."

"That is true. The world is full of hate and fear enough."

"Probably because people are too careful with the others—with love and kindness," Anja mused. "They are afraid it won't be returned in equal measure. Or afraid they will be the only one giving. Or afraid it will be unwanted. For it is not kindness to force your heart upon someone who doesn't want it, just as it is cruel to force a touch upon someone who doesn't desire it."

His short, harsh laugh startled her. "Yes," he agreed abruptly.

She bit her lip, studying his face. "It must take a lot of courage to love. But kindness doesn't need courage. So it should be easiest. Yet I do not see it as often as one would think…and am probably not kind as often as I should be."

Gruffly he said, "You journey now to slay a spider in

your mother's bedchamber, with no benefit to yourself—and despite the hardship of the journey. What is that but kindness?"

Anja laughed. "And that is very kind of you to say."

His grin flashed again and he teased her, "And very easy for me to say."

True. But not all that he did was easy. "You, too, are undertaking this journey," she pointed out. "Is that not also kind?"

His humor vanished. "I could have sent soldiers with you as escort and ordered them to kill your spider. I do not make this journey for your mother or for you, but for myself."

Puzzled by his reply, she wondered, "What do you get out of it, then?"

His grim silence was the only answer.

5

KAEL THE RAVINER

Vale

UNCEASING HUNGER. THAT WAS WHAT Kael had gotten from this. Twice he stroked his cock to completion before making his way to Anja's chamber. No longer did she latch the door when she retired for the evening; instead she left it unlocked in anticipation of his coming.

But no. Not in anticipation. He could not allow himself to mistake her actions and give them a meaning he would prefer.

She did not leave the door open in anticipation. She left it open because she knew there was no other option but to let him in, and letting him in when he arrived forced her from bed.

She did not stir when he let himself in now. The chamber was stiflingly hot. A fire smoldered in the hearth. Anja already slept, the covers barely covering her hips, as if she had kicked them away in her sleep.

Her bare legs were not an invitation.

His spent cock already stirring again, Kael gritted his teeth and stalked to the alcove at the opposite side of the chamber, which opened up to a small balcony that barely allowed for a single person upon the outcropping. This night they had not stopped in a public house as they had during every other night in their journey, but had reached the city at the far north of Vale, just before the great river that marked the border between that kingdom and Lyngfen. Word of Kael's journey had reached the city before he and Anja had, and they had been met and welcomed at the city's gates by Vale's administrator. Her residence was theirs for the night, a stone keep richly appointed.

Those appointments included a decanter of wine upon a sideboard. Though he misliked the sweetness of it, Kael helped himself to the drink before opening the balcony doors, letting the cold air sweep in.

Standing beneath the open archway and looking out into the winter's night did nothing to cool the flames within, but the wine might dull his senses enough to allow him to sleep against her.

A rustling from the bed tightened his skin. Her footsteps were light, almost imperceptible, but he was so attuned to her that she might as well have stomped her way to his side.

"This is a fine idea," she said at his shoulder. "It is unreasonably hot within."

He glanced down. She had closed her eyes. Fine perspiration glistened over her pale skin as the cold air wafted past her face. She had not donned her wolfskin before coming to his side, and her tunic was not the heavy winter covering that she normally wore, but a fine linen that skimmed her every curve—and exposed almost the full length of her legs.

"You will catch cold," he told her gruffly.

Opening her eyes, she smiled up at him. "I think not."

He could not think at all. At first sight, her beauty had pierced him like a spear though his chest. But these past days there had been new light in her face, and it shone so bright that simply looking at Anja burned her image into his eyes and his heart.

But he could not look away. And he had to remind himself that when she softly bit her bottom lip and looked shyly up at him through her lashes, it was not an attempt to allure him. So unceasing was his hunger for her, so desperate was he, Kael wanted to believe every small gesture she made was invitation to carry her to bed and sink between her thighs.

But he had told her what that invitation must be, that it must come from her mouth, not a flirtatious look.

Perhaps she didn't even know what she did.

But she likely didn't mistake the hunger in his gaze

when he looked back at her. Her smile faded slightly and her gaze averted from his.

She stroked her fingers down the lattice work of the door, a gesture that tormented him so badly that he barely heard her say, "I rarely think to open shutters or doors."

Because the wards would not work. He forced himself to stop imagining those fingers tracing the length of his cock. "It is not allowed?"

"Only rarely. And everyone within the palace must be warned first. May I?" she asked and without waiting for answer, reached for him. His heart thundered, but when she only lifted the cup from his grip he laughed at himself.

She would not knowingly touch him. But now the sweetness of the wine seemed not so unappealing, now knowing it would be the flavor upon her lips.

Lips that he would have given up a kingdom to kiss. Four kingdoms. And sought new kingdoms to conquer and give away, so he might always have another taste.

She sipped, looking out over the city. "What mountains are those in the distance? I am so turned around within this keep, I don't know the direction I'm looking in."

And in the four kingdoms, there were mountains in every direction but east. "That is south."

Grimhold and his fortress lay before them, though he could not see it at this distance and in the dark.

A faint smile touched her lips. "You seemed to be brooding mightily when I came. Do you wish yourself back at your stronghold?"

He had no response but a short laugh.

Tilting her head, she looked up at him. Curiosity tinged her voice. "Do you feel imprisoned there?"

"No." Confined, yes. "Not as I was imprisoned before, in the mines. Now I could easily break free if I wished to."

"'*Break* free'?" she echoed. "You are not free now?"

"Is any king?"

"I suppose if you see duty as a chain, then you are not. Do you?"

"No. But it is not the same freedom."

Her lips pursed as she considered that. They were not an invitation, either, but he needed a taste. Taking the wine back from her, he did not sip but downed half the remaining amount.

"You are still free," she said. "But the difference is, I think, that you have never been a leader. Alone you destroyed Geofry and his warlords—you led no army, were responsible for no one else. Now you are responsible for four kingdoms."

"That is not the only difference. I go hunting and I am surrounded by courtiers, and a huntmaster who flushes out game for me. I practice my blade against a swordmaster who will not parry in return, no matter how I goad him. I command armies I never see and lead soldiers I never fight beside."

She tilted her head, studying him. "So you are bored—need more challenge?"

"No." Nothing so paltry. "I am slowly dying. I feel I

am being smothered and coddled until I cannot move or breathe within the stronghold's walls."

"Then name a successor and leave."

He clenched his jaw and shook his head.

Her brow furrowed with concern, she asked, "Why did you accept the crown? For riches?"

"Because the people asked me to take it."

"You could have instead asked for a reward and ridden away. Is that what you wish to do now?"

"No." He wished to fuck her against the wall.

She leaned back against the frame of the archway, her breasts sweetly rounded against her tunic. Her nipples stood like berries beneath.

Those were not an invitation. They did not mean she was as aroused by his nearness as he was by hers.

Abruptly he strode back into the heated chamber, snatching a blanket. He returned and thrust it at her.

"You are cold," he said gruffly.

"I'm not."

"You are. Cover yourself."

Biting her lip, she took the blanket and wrapped it around her shoulders. He refilled his cup from the decanter, and would have filled another cup for her, but he wanted his mouth where hers had been.

He returned to the balcony and found her watching him, studying him, considering him. Trying to make sense of him.

"Why take the throne? It cannot only be because you

were asked."

"I thought I might be needed—to defend them. So they might continue to be free instead of fall under another Geofry." On a heavy sigh, he shook his head. "But I have not needed my sword. Only my seal at meetings."

"So you want to take the lazy way of ruling a kingdom."

He could not mistake the teasing note in her lilting voice but he sensed she was not entirely joking. Narrowing his eyes, he echoed, "Lazy?"

"You think that swinging a sword is a magical cure for a kingdom's ills?" Smiling, she took the cup from him again. "Ruling a kingdom is making certain the grain in the fields ends up in the bellies of your people. It is maintaining relations with other kingdoms that can affect the safety of your people and the trade that enriches their lives. It is deciding how many taxes can provide for everyone but won't take so much that they can't provide for themselves."

Grim resignation filled him. "I am better suited to a sword than deciding those things. Perhaps better suited as a conqueror than king."

"I would not agree. I have seen how you are with your people. You don't need to hammer out the details yourself but tell your ministers and advisors what you want to accomplish." She frowned slightly and raised her gaze to his. "Why do they not already handle the details? I have never seen anyone as besieged as you were the morning at your stronghold."

Besieged. Not by an enemy, but by his own advisors.

"I am told that is how it is done."

"Not in Ivermere or any other kingdom I have visited. More likely it was how Geofry did it—never relinquishing control, never letting anyone make decisions for his kingdoms."

"Better for the advisors, if that was true," Kael said. "They would have been less likely killed if they were not directly responsible for a failure."

"Fortunate, then, that your advisors do not have to fear the same from you." Thoughtfully, she sipped more wine, then said, "You can relinquish that control to others who are capable—but it is best to first learn exactly what they are in control of, so that you will know if they are handling it well."

"I think they would."

She nodded in agreement. "But the rest cannot be wholly learned from sitting on your throne and listening to reports. Better to travel through your kingdoms and see for yourself."

"Do you think they wish me to? They are afraid of me."

She looked at him in surprise, frowning. "They love you."

"Everywhere we go, they are terrified."

"At first they are," she conceded. "But by the time you leave each place, they are less afraid, because their fear is only born of uncertainty. Because they don't know what to make of you. There are so many stories of your bloodlust—"

"All true."

She tilted her head. "But you have not killed anyone

on this journey."

"I have not killed anyone since taking the throne and ridding this land of Geofry's supporters."

Her brows rose. "That long?"

No one was more surprised than he. "None have deserved it. But I have also not traveled outside the stronghold much. Perhaps I will kill more soon."

Pursing her lips again, she nodded. For a long moment silence fell between them, then she said, "I have always thought of kings and queens as parents. Perhaps because they *were* my parents—"

He laughed. "That would perhaps explain it."

She bumped her hip against his leg, companionably chiding him for his teasing. "I only mean to say that Geofry was a particularly cruel father. Any child—no matter how old—would be wary of anyone in that role now. The only thing to do is to carry on and let them see you for who you are. That you are a king who will not punish anyone unless that punishment is deserved—and you should make very clear what is deserved and not."

Was it so easy to win over people? Simply to let them see who he was.

More often than not, who he was terrified people. But Minam, who knew him best, was not afraid of him. Anja was not…he didn't think.

Never had he spoken with anyone as he had with her tonight. Never had he revealed so much. Yet he didn't know if it meant anything. Anja possessed a natural grace and kindness that he had witnessed everywhere they went, had seen her listening to troubles and treating them with care no matter how trivial or how weighty.

And after they had spoken of pure magic, he knew she had made more effort to use hers—not her corrupt magics, for as far as he was aware, she hadn't cast a spell since they had left the stronghold. But he knew she had determined to be more kind.

He wondered what she would say if he told her that he had seen no difference in her. Before and after, she was as caring with those she met. She had been bursting with magic before she'd ever known what it was.

She looked up at him curiously again. "Why haven't you left the stronghold before? You clearly enjoy traveling and seeing how your people get along. And if a threat came and you were needed to defend them, there is nowhere within your kingdoms that you cannot be reached within a fortnight."

Bitterly he shook his head. "I am told that is what a king does. He waits for his people to come to him; he does not go to them."

"Nonsense. What *you* do is what a king does. So tour your kingdoms once a year—or once a season. Demand that you hunt alone and give your swordmaster leave to do his worst. Visit your armies and, if you go to war, ride at their head. And *that* will be what a king does."

Could it be so simple? He did not know. But what she suggested sounded more suited to him. Never had he been a man to be led and coddled.

She was not done trying to persuade him. "Your advisors have good hearts and they have done their best. But they know how to help the king; they do not know how to *be* king."

He offered her a wry smile. "I'm not certain I do either."

"I think that whatever you do, you will make a fine ruler." She grinned. "Just do not take Geofry as a model."

"I will not. It would only give you more reason to kill me."

"If I thought you deserved it." Again she bumped her hip against his leg. "But I do not think you do."

If Kael took what he wanted now, he would. But had her mind truly changed so much? Could he win her, too? Would she want his touch as he wanted hers? Not dread his cruelty or merely tolerate a kiss?

Heart pounding, he cupped her face. With the soft brush of his thumb, he touched the lips stained red with wine. She went utterly still, her gaze locked upon his.

"Do you fear me, Anja?"

"No," she whispered.

But her answer trembled over his skin on a shaky breath. A shiver ran through her form, a quiver on her lips. Uncertainty flashed through her eyes.

"I think you lie," he said harshly and dropped his hand away, turning to look blindly out over the balcony. "Begone from me and return to bed."

She hesitated. "Shall I wait for you to tie me?"

Unless she also lied about what he deserved, Anja would not attempt to kill him. Though at this moment, he would not care if she did. Better death than to feel her shake with fear at his touch.

With a raw voice, he said, "No. And from this night forward, I will not share your bed."

He did not turn to see her reaction. He could not bear to witness her relief. But she must have been stunned by his decision, because for a long moment he heard nothing from her at all.

Then, with a quiet sigh, she left him alone.

6

ANJA THE LIAR

Lyngfen

SHE *HAD* LIED.

Anja had said she didn't fear him. But she did. Not that he would harm her—or harm anyone undeserving—but she feared that her heart would be sliced open when they parted.

Every time he touched her, she craved more. Every time he spoke, she wished never to stop talking with him. Every hour she spent with him, she wanted another. But not merely hours. Days. Years.

But only a week remained until she would be home.

And her lie had put distance between them. Since that night, he had not left her alone in her bedchamber—had not left her unprotected—but he slept on the floor, no matter that she implored him to take comfort beside her.

She missed his strength. She missed his warmth. She did not miss being tied—but she missed the tying, that breathless moment when he bound her. When he seemed to loom over her, dark and ravenous. When the silence between them seemed full of anticipation and the tension coiled so tight.

The tension was still there, but little silence remained. So many times she'd been reprimanded for her unguarded tongue, but now she was a slopmouth in truth, talking on and on, yet saying nothing of importance.

Because she had not the courage to say what she most wanted to. To tell him how much she wanted a kiss or a touch. Any would do. But she dared not speak when everything she told him without words was ignored. Her every alluring glance and every flirtatious gesture had been made as if to a wall. Or worse, made him turn away.

But on the road, he did not ignore her or turn away. And although the better she knew him, the more danger her heart was in, she could not stop trying to discover more.

He probably thought it was only boredom. The landscape offered little to engage the attention. Snow had fallen over the mire, then frozen hard, crusting the long, dried grasses in brittle ice. A bitter wind drove into their backs, and every time she turned her head it bit into her cheeks. This day they had met few other travelers, and their horses' tracks were the first to mark the road. Though she had traveled through this kingdom on her journey to the stronghold, she had no memory of it while sleeping. Never before had she been anywhere so bleak and desolate.

Perhaps Kael had.

"Are the Dead Lands much like this?"

He shook his head. "Too many trees grow here."

A laugh burst from her on a puff of frozen air. For there were trees—but only a few, their bare and gnarled limbs burdened with hundreds of ravens that watched them pass in eerie silence.

His smile answered her laugh but it did not last. With a lift of his chin, he gestured ahead. "That is similar."

The ruins of a walled village. They had passed through many such ruins, but unlike in the Dead Lands, it had not been a scaling that had destroyed so many homes along this road. Instead it had been Qul Wrac, who had served Geofry in Lyngfen.

It was said when Kael had first cut his corpse-strewn path from Lyngfen to Vale, that he'd carried Qul Wrac's head on the horn of his saddle. But when Anja had asked him whether it was true, he'd denied it—and said he'd carried Qul Wrac's head upon a pike, instead.

She could not see him as that bloody conqueror, though she had no doubt of its truth. Even now, he was surrounded by the tools of battle. His sword, an axe, daggers in his boots. Yet more and more, she could not imagine him in a butcherer's rage. Always he had such restraint.

Ahead, the wooden gate that had once guarded the

entrance to the village lay in splinters between the stone walls. Beyond the broken gate, the road continued through what remained of mud homes, the thatched roofs caved in.

A few hundred paces from the gate, Kael halted his horse, gaze fixed intently ahead. Immediately Anja did the same. Silently she waited—this was something he often did when they approached a point in the road where the view ahead was obstructed, or where someone might lay in wait to ambush. She didn't know exactly what he looked for—the only movement Anja could see was a scrap of cloth fluttering at the broken edge of the gate, the only sound she heard was the rustle of wind through the frozen grasses. Yet he must have heard or seen or perhaps smelled *something*.

"I feel eyes upon us," he said.

She did not. With pounding heart, she looked and listened—then gestured subtly to a twisted tree near the village wall. "Perhaps the ravens?" she whispered.

A faint smile touched his lips. "No. Come."

He nudged his horse forward, but did not go far. Instead he led her off the road, pausing near the tree she'd indicated, within a stone's throw of the old gate. "I'll ride ahead and return for you. If anyone lies in wait, it will be within the village."

Because there was nowhere else to plan an ambush. Behind them, the mire was an empty waste; not a single traveler could be seen in the distance. The only conceal-ment was offered by these ruins.

At her nod, he asked grimly, "You know spells of defense—the ones that kill?"

"I know many spells. Even one that could burst a man's eyes within his head." Anja's mother had seen that she was educated well, for all the good it did her.

"If anyone but me comes through that gate, use it. Do not fear the scaling. Your spells will not touch me."

How could he be so certain? But Kael did not wait to explain. Instead he threw the sides of his cloak back from his shoulders—to free his arms, she realized. If he drew his sword, the heavy material would not hamper his swing.

As he disappeared into the village and the sound of the hoof beats retreated, all was quiet. Then a raven cawed, the hoarse sound rubbing prickles over her unease-tightened skin. She shivered despite the heavy comfort of her coat. Beneath her, the big mare moved restlessly. She tossed her head and snorted, sending plumes of steam into the air.

And there were eyes upon her.

Anja stilled, her gaze searching. There was no one in sight. Yet whatever she had sensed—that Kael had sensed earlier—she knew with absolute certainty that it was close…and coming closer.

Sudden fear knocked her heart against her ribs. She dug her heels in and the horse sprang forward—

Then whipped around, the mare rearing and her hindquarters pivoting as if her reins had suddenly been yanked to the side. Unseated by the abrupt movement, Anja couldn't regain her balance. Her cry cut short as she crashed to the ground on a clump of frozen grass. Stunned, she lay on her side, coughing and trying to regain her breath.

"Whoa, there! Easy, girl." The deep voice was joined by another man's cackling laugh. "Easy."

Gasping air into her pained chest, Anja scrambled back toward the wall, regaining her feet and drawing her sword with hands that shook wildly.

The "easy, girl" had not been for her. A full-bearded giant of a man held her horse's reins, trying to soothe the startled animal. Four other men were with him, watching Anja with expressions that ranged from cruelly amused to darkly irritated to hotly eager. A spell, she realized. A cloaking spell of some sort had allowed these bandits to come upon her unseen.

Were there more? Had they done the same to— "Kael!" she screamed his name. "Kael!"

That drew more cackling laughter from a wiry figure standing behind a man who watched her with an amused expression. Long blond hair framed a face reddened by the wind. The bandits' leader, she thought. A leather cuirass armored his chest, a heavy cloak fell around his shoulders, and he stood with the point of his sword buried in the ground between his booted feet, hands resting lightly on the hilt in a careless pose.

His blond eyebrows arched. "Kael?" Laughing, he shook his head. "Your companion was a giant, for certain, but no bigger than my shaggy friend there—and no king. Did you see a golden crown upon his head? Perhaps there was a spell upon his crown, to disguise it as we were disguised."

He addressed the last to the dark-haired man who stood a few paces away, and who did not wait as carelessly as his leader. With crossbow braced at his shoulder, he faced the broken gate—where Kael would come through.

He cast an irritated glance back at them before resuming his watch. "Crown or not, he must still be dealt with. Hogtie his slattern and come back to her when we've finished him. It's cursed cold out here."

"You are the greatest bowman in all of the fen, Erac," the leader said. "Fly a bolt through his throat when he comes for her. Then his woman can keep you warm."

So they had not ambushed Kael while concealed by the spell. He was alive. "You are all fools," Anja said coldly. "Dead fools, now. For that warrior *is* Kael the Conqueror."

Smiling, the blond tugged his sword from the ground. "And who are you?" he asked mockingly. "His fair queen?"

She only wished it so. "I am Princess Anja of Ivermere."

"Ivermere?" His grin flashed white teeth. "Here is your princess, Ulber! Perhaps she will give your poor father pardon for his magical crimes, burn that rune from his arm, and you will all return home!"

Holding her sword in front of her, Anja spared the quickest glance to the sullen figure behind him, wearing a ragged cloak with hood drawn up.

"Ulber is not much of a spellcaster," the blond confided to her in a lower voice, slow steps carrying him closer. "He only knows a trick or two, and his mother's got no more magic in her than I do. But a princess, eh? You could crack our necks with a single word."

"That spell is five words," Anja told him, "but I have no need of it."

Not when she had firm ground beneath her feet and a wall at her back. With easy grace, Anja slipped her arms out of her coat sleeves and let the heavy wolfskin fall to the ground. Immediately the wind gnawed through her tunic, lifting the hair at her nape and slithering down her collar, but with hot blood racing through her veins, she did not feel the cold.

Without taking her eyes from the blond bandit, she kicked the fur aside so it would not tangle her feet. She arched a brow—challenging him to attack.

Behind him came another cackle. "I like this one, Nahk! I will have her after you are done."

"I'd best go last," said the bearded giant holding her horse. "You'll not get much use out of her after."

"Take my place," the spellcaster beside him said. "I would rather have her coat than fuck a ghost."

"And I want to know whether her muff's as white as her hair," Nahk said, inching closer.

Another cackling laugh. "After that old woman this summer, you've gotten a taste for gray twat."

"Then spread her thighs and get on with it!" Erac snapped at them. "He ought to have returned to her by now, and with her screaming his name we have lost the surprise."

"We need no surprise," Nahk said. "Because unless he can fly upon the wind over that stone wall, he cannot come upon us here without first exposing himself to our arrows."

So far as Anja knew, Kael could not fly. According to legend, however, after breaking his chains he had climbed an unscalable shaft within the Blackworm mines. If he had done that, then a village wall would be nothing.

But like the head upon a saddlehorn, not every detail within the stories was true. So she would not depend upon Kael to save her.

"I hear his horse," the giant said, cocking his head. "He returns through the gate."

"Well, then," Nahk said, suddenly advancing with speed. "Erac's crossbow will end him. Let the last thing he witnesses be his woman beneath us."

With cheers and laughter urging him on, Nahk aimed a heavy two-handed blow at the base of Anja's blade—clearly meaning to disarm her by knocking the sword from her grip. On light feet, she danced to the right, and as his swing carried his arms downward, leaving his neck unguarded, she sliced in an upward arc toward his throat.

His head jerked back at the last moment. A stripe opened up the side of his face, from the corner of his mouth to his ear. The cheers from the others fell silent.

Eyes wide and disbelieving, Nahk touched fingers to his bleeding cheek. No longer did he care about the color of her muff, Anja saw. Her death lay in his furious gaze when he looked to her again.

But she had no intention of dying.

He struck. Anja parried with a ring of steel on steel, the force of his blow shivering through the blade and into her arms. Swiftly she pivoted and swung low, needing to wound and slow him, for his chest was armored from shoulder to hip and a fatal strike would not be easily found there. He evaded her thrust and there was no letting up after that, only the crunch of frozen grasses beneath her feet and the crash of steel, as she parried and returned blow after blow.

Then her boot slipped on a film of ice. In a heartstopping moment, Anja's knee slammed into the ground and he came at her, swinging his blade high, preparing to bring the sharpened edge down upon her head.

With an upward thrust, she drove her sword into his abdomen, into the softness exposed beneath the waist of his cuirass. His blade made its downward swing, but with no direction and no force. His bloodied mouth opened wide in a soundless scream. He stared at her with bulging eyes, his face turning red and the veins in his temples throbbing. Anja ruthlessly shoved the blade deeper as she stood, and his sword fell harmlessly from his weakened hands. Quickly she pulled her weapon free and spun to face the others.

Hoofbeats approached, and she dared a hopeful glance—but it was only Kael's horse, no rider. The other bandits must have already seen and dismissed the riderless animal as no threat, and now stared at her with expressions of dismay, shock…anger.

"Murdering whore!" Face contorted with rage, Erac pivoted, leveling his crossbow at her heart. "You'll pray that we finish—"

A flash of steel spun through the air—Kael's battle-axe. With a wet, terrible *thunk*, Erac's head split open.

A deafening roar thundered across the mire. The ravens took to startled wing, bursting from the tree in a raucous black cloud even as Kael sprang from the high wall, slamming to the ground in a pantherish crouch. Fury lighted his eyes with deadly blue fire. His gaze swept Anja's length, lingering on the blood staining her blade, before touching upon the dying man at her feet. As if satisfied she was unharmed, he rose from his crouch on tightly coiled muscles—and drew his sword.

"There's only one of him." The bearded giant stepped forward, weapon at ready. "We'll take him together—"

Kael charged the giant.

Anja had heard stories of the Butcherer. Some from his own lips. And she had seen death before, both monstrous and gentle, and had just killed a man with her sword. But that painful death was a bloodless mercy compared to the violence of Kael's blade, and the legends had not prepared Anja for the man. Every blow rent limbs, not simply stopping the giant but destroying him in great gouts of spurting blood. No longer did his companion laugh and cackle but spilled guts onto the reddened snow, and his horrendous screams were abruptly silenced. Shouting a cloaking spell, clutching a dagger in his raised fist, the spellcaster rushed forward and vanished. Without a break in his stride, Kael jerked his axe free of Erac's skull and hurled the weapon. The spellcaster appeared again, bloodied fingers clawing at the heavy blade embedded in his chest. Staggering, he fell to his knees, and Kael ended him with a swing of his sword that cleaved head from neck.

Chest heaving, he ripped his axe free and turned toward Anja. His voice had a thick and guttural bite as he asked, "Are you hurt?"

Mutely she shook her head.

Jaw tightening, he crouched and wiped the blade of his sword on the spellcaster's cloak. "Why did you not use your magic?"

Still stunned by the carnage before her, she was unprepared to answer. She stumbled over her tongue a few times before finally giving an explanation. "I wished to test my skill with a sword."

"You are no fool, Anja," he said harshly. "But you are a liar. And—"

Abruptly he stopped, looking at her. His face darkened. Rising to his feet, he stalked toward her. Pulse racing, Anja held her ground. She had lied to him. And whatever he meant to do now, she didn't believe he would hurt—

He dropped to his knees before her. "This is *your* blood." With rough hands, he shoved the hem of her tunic upward, exposing the straps that secured her leggings to the tops of her thighs. With a single tug, that strap untied, and the heavy stocking slipped down. She sucked in a hissing breath. A slash cut across the outside of her thigh—a thrust of Nakh's blade that she had parried, but had still found a mark. But she had not even felt it until this moment.

At that hiss of breath, Kael's gaze flew to hers. So stricken was his expression that for a moment, she felt a rush of fear that the wound was far worse than it looked.

But it wasn't. If anything, it looked worse than it truly was.

"It is only a shallow cut," she whispered.

Returning his gaze to her injury, he bent his head for a better look. "It still bleeds. And it needs cleaning."

As he spoke, Kael gently cupped the column of her thigh, callused fingers sliding over the sensitive inner skin. Anja went rigid, her body responding to that touch, her senses a wild riot of stinging pain and pleasure.

Face bleak, Kael immediately withdrew his hand, his fingers leaving a bloodied mark on her skin. Spitting a foul curse, he stood and glowered down at her.

"Heal it," he commanded.

Pleasure vanished, replaced by pure pain—and dread. Silently Anja shook her head.

He bent closer and growled, "Heal it."

In a desperate whisper, she hissed, "It will scale."

"And injure a raven? Then we will roast it and eat it." Kael's mouth twisted. "Or it might finish off that dying bastard."

The bandit leader, who had not yet succumbed to Anja's blade. Instead he had been trying to escape, crawling upon the ground toward the gate, leaving a bloodied trail through the snow. He had not gotten more than a few paces.

Her heart aching, Anja yielded. "I can't heal it."

Kael stared at her with burning eyes—and abruptly left her, sweeping up the bandit's fallen sword and shoving it through the back of his leather armor and into his heart. Immediately the bandit's crawling ceased.

Trying to breathe past the ragged pain in her chest, Anja watched him continue to his horse, where he loosened the wineskin from the saddle and poured water over his hands, washing them.

With tears clogging her throat, she tugged up the stocking, feeling every painful edge of the injury as it was covered.

"Leave it," Kael barked. He was returning to her, a small ceramic jar cupped in his hand, and a wetted strip of cloth in the other. He scooped up her coat and swung it over her shoulders, for a brief moment surrounding her in his scent and warmth.

He sank to his knees again. Intending to tend her wound, she realized.

She tried to take the wet cloth from him. "I can do this—"

"With magic?" He slashed her an angry glance. "Be still."

Tears filled her eyes and she looked upward, blinking

them away. It was several moments before her raw throat felt capable of passing words through it without ripping her flesh apart.

"I'm sorry," she said hoarsely.

He flashed her another hard, sharp glance. "For what?"

"For lying." Her breath shuddered. "I've made you angry."

"I am *angry*," he ground through gritted teeth, "because I left you unprotected, with only a sword to defend yourself. And because I did not see it before. I had noted that you never used magic, and thought there might be reasons for it, but a reason I never was considered that you *couldn't*."

Angry...at himself. "But I lied. I let you believe that I was a spellcaster."

"What of it?" He gently began cleaning the blood from her skin. "What better protection for a woman than everyone believing she can burst their eyes with a spell? I do not tell my enemies all of my weaknesses or strengths. Letting them believe what they like has saved me trouble and given me an advantage many times."

An advantage such as an affinity for climbing walls. With heart pounding, she asked, "Are we enemies?"

A wry glance answered her. "I do not often share them with my allies, either."

A tremulous smile touched her mouth. An ally. She wished for far more. But she would take what he gave.

He opened the small pot. "This ointment not only has a foul smell, it will feel like fire in your wound and numb the joints in that limb—but it will keep an injury from festering."

She nodded and steeled her nerves. His blunt fingers slicked the ointment the length of the cut—and he had not been jesting. It felt as if a hot poker had been jabbed into her leg. She made a small sound, and had to brace her hand against his broad shoulder when the strength in that knee seemed to give out.

"Only a few moments," he murmured soothingly, spreading more.

"I know how long your moments are," she gritted.

He grinned. "Why do you have no magic?"

Speaking of it was more agonizing than the ointment. Yet he deserved to hear. "I was born this way."

"Are the king and queen not your parents, then?"

"They are." With a thick voice, she said, "My father could not bear my mother's pain in childbirth, so cast a spell to take it away. If I ever had any magic, the scaling of that spell stole it. It took her pain and gave it to me."

Frowning, he looked up at her. "You are always in pain?"

Bitterly she said, "What do you think my life has been? I am the only one in Ivermere without magic. Me, the princess. I am a disappointment and a shameful stain upon the realm."

"Your father is the shame."

Was he? "He did it out of love. To help her. Is that not a kindness?"

"It was selfishness, because *he* could not bear her pain. She was not dying. Instead of casting a spell to take her pain, he should have asked her if she could bear it."

"You did not ask me if I could bear this scratch."

His frown deepened as he looked up at her. "When I asked, I knew you had no magic. But if I had been wrong, I risked harming nothing but a dying bandit and a dinner. I would not risk a child. And I would not punish that child afterwards for what my spell did."

And this was why she feared him. How quickly he had taken hold of her heart. Less than a week of their journey remained. By the last day, he would have it all.

Then take it with him when he left her in Ivermere.

She could not hide her despair. But he mistook the reason for it.

"Even if you cannot cast spells, you still have great magic, Anja," he said softly. "Today I saw your courage."

She laughed, a harsh and painful sound. "Was it courage or desperation?"

He frowned. "Why do you think desperation makes it less admirable?"

"Because I had no choice. That is not courage."

"There is always a choice. You could have chosen to do nothing."

"My choice was the pain they planned for me, or the pain I might know if my sword failed. That is no choice."

"You decided which pain was more acceptable to your heart." His voice roughened. "You decided how you would live—or die. You did not let them decide for you. That is courage, too." He used strong teeth to rip a length of cloth, then said, "If people were never desperate, if there was no fear or danger, we would not need courage. Do you think I fought so much because I was content and the choice was easy? My courage has always come from desperation. That does not lessen it. Just as yours is not lessened."

Her gaze searched his face. "You are kind to me."

"Kindness is easy. Courage is not." He eyed her solemnly. "Neither is living without magic in Ivermere. I think you have more courage than I knew, Anja."

Her heart full, she could not speak. As if sensing how overwhelmed she was, he lowered his gaze to offer her privacy and slowly began wrapping the clean strip of linen around her thigh.

And it was not only her heart that was overwhelmed. Her exposed leg ought to have been freezing, yet she felt so hot—and he was so close. His fingers slipped over her skin, so carefully, almost reverently. He had said the ointment had a foul smell yet he seemed to be leaning in toward the juncture of her thighs, breathing deep, and she felt a great strain within the muscles beneath her hands.

By the gods, and what she imagined then—of lifting the hem of her tunic and exposing bare flesh beneath. Of urging him closer, until his mouth met the part of her that burned hotter than any wound. The part of her that was so wet, her inner thighs felt the icy kiss of the wind more sharply than the rest of her skin, and she was uncertain whether the ointment was all that slicked his fingers. But she could pull him forward, and know the kiss and the touch she so desperately craved.

Unless he turned away again.

He suddenly stilled, and looked up to her with eyes that seemed to burn with hunger.

Anja trembled as a war waged within her. She had not enough courage to pull him closer, not enough courage to face his rejection again. This gentle touch as he tended to her might be all she would ever know of him. But from now until they reached Ivermere, perhaps she could have the small joy of touching him.

Her fingers slipped over his upturned face, tracing the sharp lines of his cheekbones. "There is blood here. Do you wish me to wash it for you?"

Catching her fingers, he shook his head. "I have blood everywhere upon me," he said gruffly. "And it doesn't wash."

He did not mean the crimson staining his skin. "Will mine?"

"This was no stain upon you. It is their stain."

The bandits'. "Then this blood on your face and hands is their stain, too. You wear the stains of many villains."

Smiling, he pressed a kiss to her fingers. She caught her breath, in pleasure and hope, but he only rose to his feet.

"You are cold," he said, folding her hands between his. "Let us ride to find a warm inn and a hot meal."

"What of them?" She glanced at the bandits' bloodied remains.

"The ravens will make use of them."

With that, he swept her up and lifted her astride the mare. And as she gathered up her reins, Anja knew her heart would not be merely sliced open when this was done. Instead it would be rended into bloodied pieces, left as carrion.

That was what the Conqueror did.

7

KAEL THE WOLFKILLER

Lyngfen

FROM ALMOST EVERY CORNER OF his kingdoms, Black-worm Mountain loomed visible in the distance. As they'd traveled north on this journey, it had always lain in front of them. Now it no longer lay ahead, but rose to the west as they passed through the upper part of Lyngfen.

Fifteen years he had spent in the belly of that mountain, in the mines and tunnels that seemed a sunless world of their own. A world that Kael had destroyed almost the very moment after he'd freed those who'd been enslaved there.

Yet it was not those fifteen years that loomed in his mind when the mountain was no longer a peak in the distance but a glowering hell nearby. Instead it was the cursed road ahead and the next four days that gnawed with vicious teeth upon his heart.

In four days, they would be in Ivermere.

"Kael."

Immediately his gaze went to Anja's face, searching for the source of the worry that sharpened her tone. She was frowning, but not looking at him. Instead she leaned over in the saddle and watched the horse's long and even stride.

"Is she favoring a leg? Her head bobs more than usual but I can't feel it in her gait."

He studied the mare's walk. "Not one leg over the other."

"Perhaps she's favoring two." Anja drew on her reins and swiftly dismounted.

Kael halted his own mount and joined her, taking Anja's reins and remaining at the mare's head while she ran her hands down the horse's forelegs.

"It's hot and swollen here." Gently she prodded the horse's leg below the knee. Nickering, the mare shifted her weight away from Anja's touch. "And the other side, too. Splints, I think."

Which would heal, given time. But they did not have much of that.

Anja let out a relieved breath, then smiled up at him. "I feared worse. Especially after that bearded bandit caught hold of her so roughly."

"That might have helped the splints along, but it was more likely the road." They had been traveling long distances each day.

Gnawing her lip, Anja rose to her feet. "I should not ride her. It is only more weight for her to carry."

"Ride with me, then." His own horse was sound and he traveled light. If he and the horse had been dressed in full armor, the chainmail and metal plating would have weighed more than she did. "The next village isn't far. We'll stable her there and leave word for the caravan that follows. By the time your trunks are delivered to Ivermere and the caravan returns this way, she'll be sound enough for the journey home."

Anja nodded, though unhappiness passed through her eyes—and he wasn't certain whether it was mention of her going home or the idea of riding with him. But he only had four days left and would not pass this opportunity to hold her again.

After tethering the mare's lead to his saddle, he moved to lift her onto his horse but she hesitated, moving back.

"If I am to ride behind you, I should mount second," she said.

"You will be in front."

She narrowed her eyes. "That is not the usual way of riding double."

"No." But he would do it no other way. If she sat ahead of him in the saddle, he would see any threat approaching. His body would shield her from any unseen threat from behind. "It is how a king rides double."

Her soft lips smashed together as if fighting a smile—a

battle she quickly lost. Laughing, she shook her head.

"I should never have told you that whatever you do is what a king does. Will you use it to get your way every time?"

"If I must."

"All right, then." But she didn't step forward to mount the horse; instead she took off her coat and turned it backward, pushing her arms back through the sleeves and covering her front in fur. At his curious look, she explained, "It is too thick and would bunch between us."

So it would. He hefted her up into the saddle, clenching his teeth against a tortured groan when she swung her leg over and he glimpsed the barest bit of skin at her inner thigh. Then she settled and straightened her tunic beneath her, so that bare skin would not chafe against leather. His cock stiff as a sword, he swung into the saddle.

She could not mistake the hardness behind her, for with both of them in the cradle of the saddle, the seat was a snug fit. His cock was a rigid pole pressing against her ass, yet she gave no indication that she noticed it—neither pressing against him or moving away. Though perhaps she didn't feel it through her thick tunic and his straining breeches. Or perhaps she believed he was always in this state, for his cock was always hard when he held her close.

By the gods, he had missed this. He had not held her since he'd stopped sharing her bed. The sweet pleasure of binding her leg had been dulled by the shame of wanting to fuck her even while she bled from an injury he ought to have prevented. And she touched him so often of late, but that was more torment, because they were innocent touches to his hands or his face.

But never did she open her mouth and ask for more.

He would have given anything she asked for. At her command, he would have razed Blackworm Mountain itself. But for now she only leaned back against his chest, her head resting on his shoulder. The coat draped like a blanket down her front and was long enough to cover their legs.

Her soft laugh shook gently through his chest. "This is quite comfortable, in truth. I could nap here."

"I will not let you fall if you do." Already he held her securely, the reins in his right hand and his left arm wrapped around her waist.

"I am not tired."

He heard the smile in her voice when she answered, yet despite how often she'd talked these past days, she seemed content with silence now.

As was Kael, though it was all he was content with. To have her against him, to know the soft feel of her, to breathe the sweet smell of her—never had he been so overwhelmed with need.

And this journey would be all that he ever had of her. He ought to have spent every moment like this, holding her close.

She reached up, and the soft touch of her fingers against his jaw thundered through his veins. Gently she turned his gaze to the west. "That is Blackworm Mountain, is it not?"

"It is."

She said nothing after that, but let her palm curl back around his nape—as if in comfort.

A comfort he didn't need, but would take. "Ask me," he told her. "I know you have wanted to all day."

She sighed, and he was sorry he'd spoken when she slid her hand from his neck and let if fall back to her lap. "I don't want to dredge up painful memories."

"It does not." There had been pain, but he had survived. That was all that truly mattered. "But there is little to say. It was as bad as you likely imagine."

"Probably worse than I *can* imagine."

Kael could imagine worse than he had suffered. He had seen worse. "I was enslaved as a boy and became a man within the mountain—and if the Dead Lands were the fire that created me, the mines hammered me into sharpened steel. Others were not so fortunate. When stories of the mines are told, it should be theirs. For they still suffer and I do not, and it's too easy to believe there were no other consequences when the story most frequently told ends in victory."

"With you killing Toatin Zan and Geofry losing his head?"

And his guts. And everything else. "Yes."

Nodding, she fell quiet for a moment, then said, "Have you ever returned to the Dead Lands?"

"There is nothing for me to return to."

She made a soft noise and her hand found his at her waist, lacing their fingers together. Another comfort he didn't need but would take. "You had a story before that, though, didn't you? You have been called the Wolfkiller—were called that even before you began your campaign against Geofry. It is said that you killed five wolves with your bare hands when you were only four years of age. That the pack had bedeviled your clan for a full winter before attacking. And while the adults were fighting them off, more cunning wolves stole into the village from the opposite direction, slinked into your hut and dragged you off to be eaten, but you killed them and escaped."

Kael grinned against her hair. "It was not my bare hands. I used a rock."

"Oh, come now!"

"Truthfully." Partially.

She scoffed.

Laughing, Kael said, "I will show you the scars on my arm from where I was dragged. They are clearly from a wolf's teeth."

"Then I will believe you killed *one*."

That would be closer to truth. So was this. "I spread the tale *and* the name—along with the name of the Butcherer. It is always an advantage when enemies fear you long before you arrive to kill them." Wryly he added, "Perhaps I did it too well."

"You speak of how the people fear you?"

"I do."

Emphatically she shook her head, her white braid whipping against his shoulder. Her fingers tightened on his as if not to allow him escape from what she said next. "As someone whose life has been saved by your butchery, I will tell you that it puts the savagery in a different light. To only *hear* of it…in truth, you sound like a monster. But upon the road, as horrible as it was, I only felt gratitude when I saw what you did to those bandits. Your people feel the same. Whether you freed them from the yoke of slavery or from Geofry's reign of terror, they know they have been saved and are grateful."

Her fingers might as well have taken hold of his throat, his tongue. Kael knew not what to say.

"Let me ask you," she said now, "why do you always remind them of your savagery? Such as at the sentencing—you made certain to describe what you did to Qul Wrac. But you do not revel in the memory, like hunters sharing stories around a fire. And with me, you do the same. Often because I ask, but you do not spare the gory detail."

Grimly he replied, "I do it so there is no mistaking who I am."

"But you only give one part of who you are. The bloodiest part. You almost never speak of courage and strength. Never the part that the people want to celebrate: of freeing them, of inspiring them, of giving them hope."

He frowned—but again, he could not answer. This

was not a view he had of himself.

Turning her head, she leaned sideways so she could look up into his face. Her own expression was one of wonder. "You do not even realize that is how they see you? Or you don't accept it," she said thoughtfully. "Or think you do not deserve it."

That he could answer. "I'm not certain I do."

"*Your people* have decided you do. Trust them." Her eyes brightened with amusement. "How strange to think that you doubt yourself. The more powerful someone is, the more certain they usually are of their worth—and their estimate usually inflated. Do you think because of the blood on your hands, the savagery that put it there, that you are some kind of monster who deserves to be ousted and alone?" She shook her head and answered her own question before he could. "I have seen monsters. You are not one."

She said it with sheer conviction that allowed no argument, but Kael did not care to argue about himself, anyway. "What monsters have you seen?"

Her cheeks colored slightly and she pulled back against his chest again. He could not see her face but she snuggled in so sweetly from hips to shoulders that it was a fair exchange.

Every step the horse took stroked his cock against her ass, a rhythm that was pleasure and torment in equal measure. Mostly likely he would spill his seed before this ride was finished.

His only regret would be that it wasn't inside her.

"In Scalewood." She leaned her head back against his shoulder again, turned her face so that every breath was a white cloud past his jaw. "Even though I had no magic, I still wished to be useful. And there are threats that are impervious to spells and must be fought with weapons, instead. So I believed that, as a future queen, I should know how to protect my people—from the creatures within Scalewood or from monsters abroad. Like Geofry."

"Or me."

He caught the curve of her smile. "Yes. At one time, I thought Ivermere would be your next conquest."

"So you dreamed of killing me even before you decided to become my bride."

She laughed. "Yes." Her hand squeezed his again. "But this was before you began making your names across the four kingdoms. My parents wished me only to study magic and learn the workings of our kingdom. But I begged the Mistress of the Hunt to teach me the sword and more."

The hunters who destroyed the magical beasts that broke through Scalewood's wards. Just as spellcasters did, the monsters had a natural protection against magic—but instead of being resistant to the scaling, they were resistant to spells cast.

"And she agreed?" Then taught her well, by what Kael had seen.

"Yes. And that training was not *secretly* done, but my parents never liked to hear of what I did—and of course studying always came first. So it always seemed very… private."

She seemed unhappy with that word, yet Kael understood well enough. Learning the sword and hunting was something that she'd loved and was *hers*.

And there was a wistful note in her voice as she continued, "So I rode with the hunters when I could—and that was almost always at night, when my other duties were finished. Usually we patrolled the borders of Scalewood and I saw many monsters then, but they never passed the wards. All of Ivermere holds them, did you know?"

Kael nodded. Every ward had to be maintained by a spellcaster or its power faded over several days—and that ward was only as strong as the sorcerer who cast it. But it could be cast by more than one. So it did not surprise him that all of Ivermere held the wards; it would be suicide not to.

"Yet something escaped?"

"Yes. There began attacks on villages near the wood. Just…slaughter. And the bodies partially eaten. But we didn't know at first that it *was* one of the Scalewood beasts. No one saw anything of the like, and others reported seeing a man during the attacks."

"The human sort of monster." In his experience, more common than the magical sort.

"So we believed. But it wasn't. It was a wolf who could cast a transformation spell and shed his skin, then pass through the wards—because they allow humans through."

Her fingers tightened on his. "When we came upon him the first time, he'd butchered a family—and though his skin was still off, we could see he wasn't a man. Not with those claws and teeth. And we chased him. But he passed back through the wards and put on his wolfskin, and we didn't dare pursue him into the wood."

"But you knew what he was, then."

She nodded. "So we waited for him to come out again. Every hunter in Ivermere was there—and he was *so* fast and strong. Not like a man at all. We used spelled arrows that never missed their mark, yet they barely slowed him. And when hunters came close with their swords…" She let out a long sigh. "There were many killed that night. We feared that he would reach his skin and we would have to do it all over again, but the Mistress of the Hunt finally got close and beheaded him. He did not heal from that."

"Because a severed head can't cast a healing spell."

A soft breath of laughter escaped her. "No," she agreed, then lifted her arm and indicated her sleeve. "This is him. We dared the forest long enough to collect his skin, and divided it equally between the hunters who'd chased him that night. There were thirty of us in all."

Yet her coat was as long and generous as a giant's cloak. Truly a monster. "You deserve that name," he said. "Anja the Wolfkiller."

By the turn of her head, he could see the barest hint of a sad smile as she ruffled her fingers through the thick gray fur. "It was my last hunt. I was forbidden by my parents after that. It was too dangerous for a princess, the heir to the crown." Her voice caught thickly. "But not very long ago, the council took my crown anyway."

Tension gripped him. "Who took your crown? And… you are Ivermere's heir?"

"No longer. Did you not wonder why the only daughter of a king and queen would leave her realm to marry elsewhere?"

In truth, he had not. "None of my kingdoms came by inheritance. So I did not even think that yours might."

She laughed. "No. I suppose you wouldn't."

"Who took yours?"

"The High Council of Ivermere." She tipped her head back against his shoulder again, and her throat worked before she continued, "My parents fought the decision. They had seen to my education; I knew all there was to know about spells and potions and ruling Ivermere. But the council determined that anyone without magic could not claim the throne—and neither can anyone in my line, though it's entirely possible that this curse would not afflict any children I have. So the crown will pass to a cousin instead. And my parents were…so shamed. Devastated that their line would end."

He could not bear the pain he heard in her voice, the tears that were unshed but that dripped from every word. "I will take Ivermere's crown for you."

She gave a watery laugh, shaking her head. "There is no one in Ivermere who wants to see me wear it. Even my parents, it was only a matter of pride—if they'd ever had another child I'd have been shunted aside. And I see no point in fighting so hard for a place there, when they will never want me. Especially not after I have seen the people of your kingdoms, and how they love you. I would be forever yearning for that, instead."

Yearning to be wanted, but not yearning for *him*. "I would give to you Lyngfen," he said, gesturing around them, "but it is a worthless swamp."

She laughed again, and this time there was a true, merry note within the sadness. Then she drew another breath and said, "But now I recall why I told that story—and it was about your people fearing you or loving you, and whether you deserve the second."

By the gods, his Anja was tenacious. "You do not have to—"

She ran roughshod over his protest. "*And I have seen a monster*, Kael. I have seen his glee as he killed innocents, how uncaring he was of the pain left behind. I have seen how he reveled in his cruelty, and in their agony and fear. And I have seen you butcher men, but there was no glee. No revelry. Rage, for certain, but they had earned it. You are not a monster; you are a man who makes certain that what needs to be done *is* done. You are simply very… thorough."

Undisputedly so. "I will place that on my seal beside my other names," he said dryly. "'Kael the Thorough.' Not a gut left intact, not a limb left unhacked."

She nodded primly. "Not a skull left uncracked."

A breath passed, then she giggled, and Kael's own laughter roared out across the fen, shaking him so hard that he had to grasp the saddlehorn and wrap his arm tighter around Anja so they didn't tumble to the ground. Her fingers clasped his wrist as she bent forward, her body quaking and her ribs expanding as she gasped for air, then lost every breath to another bout of laughter.

Then she sat up again, and the movement was a long stroke down the length of his cock. Kael's laughter was silenced, choked by a stifled groan. Anja abruptly went still, her fingers clenched around his forearm, her entire body trembling and tense.

Imagining what Kael did? That his hands would slide into the open back of her coat and cup her breasts, find her nipples hard and ripe. Or that his fingers would slip between her legs and tease her clit until she was wet and ready to take him. That he might grip her hips, and lift her, and fill her sultry sheath with his length, and they would rock together, slowly, until she found her release and he filled her with his seed.

Though he could not do that. A virgin was she, and he would not take her upon a horse. Not the first time.

And a virgin was she, so the same thoughts were not likely what held her so still. For certain she gave no indication that she wanted anything more. She only trembled and waited. For his cock to subside?

She would have to wait forever.

His forearm an iron band around her waist, he dragged her against his chest again, as snug as they had been. She made a small sound—of dismay or disappointment—and when she tipped her head back against his shoulder, her cheeks were flushed and her breath came in soft pants.

Yet although he wished it with all of his being, she didn't turn her head and place those panting lips against his throat. Didn't look up at him with want in her gaze. Didn't give an invitation, and he could not know if this was arousal or if she was simply overheated beneath her coat.

Instead she closed her eyes and trapped her lower lip between her teeth, and remained that way for what seemed an endless time. A village was visible in the distance when she finally let go a shuddering breath and asked softly, "What name would you take, if you had only one?"

He did not even have to think. "Kael the Free."

A soft smile curved her mouth and she looked down the road, her dark eyes contemplative. "Do you think I might be happy here in your kingdoms, if I leave Ivermere?"

Sudden hope filled his chest. "Why would you return here?"

For him?

"Because there is nothing for me in Ivermere."

Not for him. "Is that why you answered the call for a bride?"

"Yes. It seemed suitable. I was raised to be a queen. But I can be useful in other ways. As a hunter, perhaps."

He frowned. Being a queen was only *suitable*? Had it

not been what she wanted?

"You said that you wanted what I had," he reminded her. "You did not mean my kingdoms?"

"I suppose it is more precise to say that I wanted to do what you had done—and you made a place for yourself." The curve of her sad smile was like a scythe slicing through his chest. "I meant to carve out a place for myself, too. Even if I had to carve out your heart first."

She had made a good start. That organ was no longer his own. She had already taken it. "I carved out my place with my sword," he told her. "It was a fine plan to use your blade to kill me to gain the same."

She turned her head against his shoulder, hiding her face from him. "But you do not want a bride."

No. He did not want a bride. He wanted Anja. And if she ever showed a hint of desire, a sign of wanting him in return—a desire not seduced or forced from her, but freely given—then he would marry her in an instant.

But she gave no indication, no invitation. She didn't want *him*. She wanted a place where she fit.

He could give that to her. Again that hope rose. He could give her a place close to him—and slowly win her heart as she had so quickly won his.

And he would rather any torment than never seeing her again. Even the torment of having her near, knowing she would never want him in return.

"After we have killed the spider, return to Grimhold with me. There is room for you in the stronghold and plenty to do."

With a startled gaze, she glanced up at him. "I am not a sorceress. So I wouldn't be of much use to you in your court."

"Just as well, for I have no use for a sorceress. Only a ward-keeper, and I have one already." And he cared not at all what she did, except that she obviously wanted to have purpose. "You should come as my…royal advisor. Already you have served me better in these past ten days than they have in over a year. So I would rather have you than the fools around me now."

A smile tugged at her lips and a hopeful light brightened her dark eyes. Her gaze moved down the road again, but he didn't think she looked at anything—instead she chewed her lip in quiet contemplation.

After a long moment, she asked quietly, "Do you think you will ever marry?"

Only if she would ever have him. "I don't know."

"I suppose…" She hesitated, and her breath stuttered before she finished, "I suppose you have no need for a wife. There must be many women in the stronghold who would see to your…needs."

"There are." Though he had no interest in touching them. Only her. Never again would he want anyone as he did Anja.

"Oh." That small reply was followed by a long silence in which she did not look back at him. She let go of his forearm and hugged her middle, as if cold beneath that long coat. Finally she continued in a thick voice, "It is very kind of you to offer. But I do not believe there is a place for me there."

No place with *him*.

She had once said there were things worse than death. Kael had not believed it then, for despite all that he had suffered, death seemed far worse. But now he understood. For he had only thought of physical suffering. He hadn't known the depths of pain a heart could feel—and whatever torments were worse than death, he would know them all when he let her go.

If he let her go. And if he did not, may the gods forgive him for not heeding her choice, because after he chained her to his side, Kael didn't think Anja ever would.

But better to have her hate him than not to have her at all.

8

ANJA THE UNKISSED

Dryloch

WHEN ANJA HAD SEEN THE public inn where they would stay the night, she had wanted to keep riding. For it was Midwinter's Eve, and the music and sounds of revelry from inside struck painful discordant notes across her shattered heart. But there was nowhere else to go. This was the last village before the Scalewood passage.

Tomorrow they would ride through that dark forest and arrive in Ivermere.

Anja sensed the celebratory mood suited Kael no better than it did her, though he didn't say so. These past days, they had spoken little. She had felt too battered inside to risk a conversation that might hurt her more than she could survive, and Kael had lapsed into a brooding silence. Every day, he held her close, for they still rode double. He had not seen another horse that he thought was worth purchasing. Anja had seen many suitable horses, but had not spent her gold on them or argued in favor of one. Instead she'd hoarded every last moment she had with him.

Even though his mood was so dark, and his body always taut with frustration. She thought the cause might be the eternally swollen size of his manhood—but never did he suggest that she might ease his arousal. He never mentioned his arousal at all. Perhaps because she was not the reason for it. He hadn't wanted her for a bride, so he likely didn't want her as a bedpartner, either.

And perhaps because he might find that partner here.

As they had been at every place they'd stopped, immediately they were offered bedchambers—but were apologetically told that the chambers were not ready for immediate occupation. So Anja could not hide as she wanted to, but found a table where she could sit and wait, her mood as dark and heavy as Kael's had been.

Had been, because upon entering the tavern, he'd recognized men—also former slaves—he'd once known in the Blackworm mines. Now he sat with them at a table across the room, and laughed with them, and drew appreciative female looks from every direction—appreciation that was mixed with the fear and apprehension that Kael initially inspired everywhere he went. But here were also people who knew him, and because he was trusted and liked by them, the women's fears would not likely last long. No doubt they would work up the courage to approach him, to offer their invitations, and extend that appreciation to his bed.

Anja had more to offer than gratitude. Because unlike these women, she *knew* him. Not just the stories, but knew his rage and his worries and his kindness. So why did she never offer an invitation?

But she knew why. He'd rejected her once. She couldn't survive his rejection again.

And she couldn't survive seeing him with another woman.

A hand settled on her shoulder and an unfamiliar voice said, "Here you have been hiding— Oh!"

Startled, Anja looked up into a wrinkled face surrounded by hair almost as white as her own.

The older woman chuckled, and returned her gnarled hand to her cane. "Forgive me. I mistook you for my sister, but I was only partly wrong. You are not Tessa. A sister, however, you might be."

Anja smiled warmly. "Sit with me, then. If your sister searches for you, she cannot miss two white heads together. I am Anja."

The woman grinned and carefully eased her thin form into the seat beside Anja's. "Thank you."

"The company will do me well, and so the gratitude is mine." A conversation would hopefully bring her out of this sour, hurtful mood—and she could not mistake the woman's guttural accent, even thicker than Kael's. "You are from the Dead Lands?"

The other woman nodded, her keen eyes studying Anja's face. "And you are from Ivermere," she said. "But clearly you do not belong to them."

Her quick blue gaze cast a significant glance across the room at Kael.

The woman was mistaken. Anja didn't belong to him, either. But it would hurt too much to confirm it out loud.

But there was no reason to say anything. A loud cheer from across the room drew their attention, and a group of villagers burst into a bawdy song about a maiden's Midwinter wish.

A song Kael knew well, she saw, when he joined in.

Beside her, the old woman sighed happily. "It warms my heart to see so many come together for Midwinter. Much has changed over the years, but that has not."

"Did you also celebrate Midwinter in the Dead Lands?" Anja could not imagine it. Midwinter was a time of cheer, and everything she'd ever heard of that land said that no happiness lived there.

But then, much had been said of Kael, too—and not all of it was true.

"We do, though since the Reckoning, not in the same way as our people once did. It is said that the Midwinter celebrations used to be as they are here. In these days, however, all the clans come together, and those who do not have enough to live through the cold bare season say what is most needed—and if the other clans have it, it is shared among all. Those clans with plenty do not ask for anything, but only make their Midwinter wishes. And if all of the clans lack the same thing, then they share that burden and fear, and none are alone in their suffering."

"So 'they shared their plenty and they shared their sparsity,'" Anja quoted softly. "That is part of a Midwinter song. The stories of ancient Midwinter celebrations sound similar to those in the Dead Lands now."

"Well, it was not the first Reckoning the world has known. Nor will it be the last."

Perhaps the next would be closer to home than Anja liked to imagine. "In Ivermere, everyone has plenty, yet still asks for gifts, as well as making their Midwinter wishes."

"If there is plenty, there is no harm in asking. And there is never harm in giving…or wishing." Her eyes twinkled merrily. "Though I wonder how often Midwinter wishes come true in Ivermere, when it is only through pure magic that they are granted."

Pure magic. Struck by a sudden realization, Anja laughed aloud.

The old woman smiled at her. "Now you must share in the thought that made you laugh. And that will be the Midwinter gift you give to me."

It was probably what this woman already knew. "That is why wishes can't be said out loud, isn't it? Because when they are spoken aloud, they become a spell, and a spell is corrupt magic."

Pleasure wreathed her wrinkled face. "So that one has taught you something of real magic."

"Yes." Grinning, she glanced at Kael, then her heart seemed to rend in two when she saw the pretty maid who had sidled up to him during the song. He did not seem to pay her any attention, but soon the song would end and she might speak to him.

And she would likely be the first of many who tried.

Throat burning, she tore her gaze from the painful scene and hoarsely asked the woman, "Do you know much about true magic, then?"

"I would think so." She eyed Kael, then Anja's stricken face, but said nothing of what she concluded of the situation between them. "I am the witch of our clan."

Shock cut through Anja's misery and she stared at the woman with jaw dropped. She had heard that term before, but only said in the most derogatory way.

As if amused by Anja's reaction, the woman chuckled. "In the Dead Lands, that is no insult. It only means that I am a…" She lifted a gnarled hand as if searching for the word. "Not a priestess, because I do not commune with gods. But I oversee births and conduct ceremonies—and heal when I must."

Heal? "You are a spellcaster?"

Her grimace deepened the wrinkles around her mouth. "When I must," she said again. "Better to heal without spells, if it can be done."

"Yes," Anja agreed softly. Just as Kael had said, too. And the maid had gone away from him but already another woman had slipped closer. "Do you know much about love?"

"I do. I know how it burns so strong and bright that it can seem to give off its own light. And you shine like the sun, Anja of Ivermere," the old woman said. "But I see shadows, too."

Eyes burning, Anja shook her head. "I don't think it can be love. It doesn't feel bright and pure. It feels like poison inside me."

"Ah." Smiling, the woman said, "Because that is not love. It is jealousy."

That could not be the only reason. "But it is not only the women. When I think that I might not see him again, I feel such pain."

"That is also not love. Love begets no pain."

"Then what is it? Because it feels like a knife in my chest."

"It is longing. Dread. Perhaps fear." The older woman's gaze burned into Anja's. "Love and kindness are the most powerful of all magics—and not only for the one who gives, but also for whom the magic is bestowed upon. So love is nothing to dread or fear."

Excruciating pressure built within her chest. On a strained whisper, she asked, "What if it's not returned?"

"Do you give a gift expecting one in return? Or do you give it for the happiness it gives?"

"What if it doesn't make him happy? What if it means

nothing at all?"

"Then hope he knows kindness, too," the old woman said, her voice warm with sympathy. "Love gives the most. But it also takes the most."

"I fear it will leave me with nothing."

The woman patted Anja's hand. "Fear is also a strong magic. As is courage. So tell me, Anja of Ivermere—which magic will you wield?"

Eyes filled with tears, Anja shook her head. "I don't know." A watery laugh escaped her. "Perhaps when I'm desperate enough, I'll find my courage."

"You seem desperate enough now," the old woman said dryly, but did not wait for a response. Instead she braced her cane against the floor and rose to her feet. "And there is my sister, waving at me to come to her. Merry Midwinter, Anja."

"Merry Midwinter…" She had not asked the woman's name. But the opportunity passed, because when she raised her head her gaze caught Kael's—and she realized belatedly that her eyes still shimmered with tears. Hastily she wiped them away, but his face had already darkened and he was striding toward her, and the old woman was moving away.

"What happened?" he demanded. "You're crying."

"I'm well. I was only talking to…that woman there." Anja spotted her in the crowd and pointed in her direction.

Kael's eyes narrowed after her. "Is that a witch?"

She almost flinched at the term. But to him, or anyone

from the Dead Lands, it apparently was not a curse but a title of honor. "It is."

Kael abruptly grinned. "We are all fortunate, then. When anyone of such powerful magic is near, Midwinter wishes are more likely to be granted."

He sounded truly elated by the prospect. And when he didn't return to his friends but took the seat the old woman had vacated, Anja's heart filled at his very nearness.

"What have you wished for?" she asked him.

But of course he would not say. Instead he laughed and shook his head.

"What gift would you ask for, then?" she wondered. "You are the ruler of four kingdoms, and a man of plenty. Yet there must be something you need. So what would you ask of me for your Midwinter gift?"

His intense gaze caught hers. His voice was gruff as he said, "Forgiveness."

Brow creasing, she searched his face, and tried to think of anything he'd said that required it. "For what?"

"For something I haven't done yet."

She huffed out a laughing breath. "Consult me when you do, then, and I will consider it." Abruptly she bit her lip. "But you had best do it by tomorrow. After that I will be in Ivermere."

"Don't be so certain," he said before sprawling back in his seat and extending his powerful legs. "And what gift would you like from me? Dryloch, Vale? My stronghold?"

Nothing so big…nothing so small.

Heart pounding in her throat, she recalled how he had described magic: an unseen force that changed the world. Anja wanted a different world than the one she had. She only needed a bit of courage.

But when she reached for that courage, she found more than she'd known. It was waiting, bold and full, for her to use.

"A kiss," she told him. "I want a kiss."

And although he was a man of sudden and volatile action, Kael did not move at all. Instead he stared at her, as if not entirely certain he'd heard. "A kiss from *me?*"

"Yes."

His eyes narrowed. "Why want something you would only tolerate?"

She *had* said that once. "That was when I didn't know you. But now it is something I desire." Her courage faltered slightly when still he didn't move, and she added on a whisper, "Very much."

Slowly, he straightened up from his sprawl, bracing his feet on the floor and leaning forward in his chair with his eyes locked on hers. "And the touch of my hands, you want that?"

Her breath shuddered. "*So* very much."

A fire seemed to light behind his eyes. "My mouth upon your tits? My tongue on your clit?"

At his shocking words, sheer need gripped her inner muscles achingly tight, and she gasped her reply. "Yes."

His scarred knuckles whitened, fingers wrapping

around the arms of his chair as if preparing to push out of it—or trying to keep himself in. "And my cock deep inside you?" His voice was a growl. "You want that, too, Anja? You want me to fuck your virgin cunt and fill you with my seed?"

So badly she couldn't speak. Only nod, her face flaming, her most intimate flesh so wet that she could feel the moisture pooling at the juncture of her thighs.

All at once he bounded out of his seat, those tightly coiled muscles releasing their tension—and carrying him past her chair in long, powerful strides. In disbelief, she whipped around. He had already reached the door leading outside, his path clearly marked by the startled villagers who were staggering in his wake.

Then he was gone. Leaving her alone.

Leaving a great emptiness where her heart had been.

Because she'd mistaken everything. She'd thought he'd only said those things because he wanted them, too. But he must have been asking the extent of the Midwinter gift she wanted from him. And he must not have wanted to give them in return…because he hadn't been able to escape fast enough.

Anja the Unwanted.

Blinded by tears, she turned away, unable to bear seeing that empty doorway. Unable to bear any of this. Being unwanted had always hurt, but never had it destroyed her. And destroyed she had been. Every breath seemed like a knife stabbing into the gaping wound that was left in her chest, the remains of a heart that had been butchered.

A commotion slowly filtered through the haze of devastation. Then Kael's irritated bellow ripped the haze away.

"Cease your struggles, witch! And put away that stick, crone, or by the gods, I will—"

A solid *thwack* cut him off and his shouted curse echoed through the inn. Through Anja's tear-blurred vision, a mountain seemed to be coming her way—a mountain with a crow flapping wildly around his head. In his arms he carried the old woman. Another white-haired woman, who must have been her sister, chased after him, hitting his head and shoulders with her cane.

With lips pursed sourly, the witch told him, "I would have come. No need to carry me as a child."

"You did not move fast enough." His burning gaze shot across the room and met Anja's. "Only you can give me a wife this night—and I need to bed my bride."

His bride. *His bride.*

The tears Anja had been trying to hold back began pouring down her cheeks.

"You do not even have a red ribbon!" the sister crowed, whacking his shoulder. "There can be no binding without one."

Shouting again, Kael spun to address the gathering crowd. "I need a red ribbon! Does anyone have a ribbon—"

Someone called that they had one, but Anja didn't see who it was. Suddenly Kael was standing before her and he was all that she saw.

Carefully, he set down the old woman. The next moment Anja's cheeks were cupped in his rough palms, his thumbs wiping away her tears.

"Are you not happy?" he asked softly. "It is more than you asked for, but if you wish for me to give your gift, then you must first give this to me."

"I cry because I *am* happy." A watery laugh escaped her. "And a Midwinter gift should not be offered with a condition attached."

"It is how a king gives a Midwinter gift."

Giggling, she shook her head. From somewhere a red ribbon was waved in their direction. Kael took the length of crimson and handed it over to the witch.

"Asking for ribbons and wives," Anja teased him. "Is that what a king also does? The man with the most plenty, also asking for the most gifts."

"The most plenty?" His gaze caught hers, shining with intense blue fire. "Without you, Anja, I have nothing."

The response took her breath away. She could only stare at him, her heart whole again—and so very full.

His gaze never leaving her face, he told the witch, "Marry us. Right here. Right now."

Her eyes sparkling, the witch said, "Put your hands together for the binding."

They both towered over the older woman, though Kael far more than Anja. Facing him, Anja held up her hand. His palm met hers, so much larger, yet still their fingers aligned and the witch slowly wove the ribbon between them.

Over her gray head, Kael asked, "Do you still intend to kill me in our wedding bed?"

Anja grinned. "No."

"I do not care if you do," he said, "as long as I have you first. I will kiss you this night, Anja. No inch of your skin will be left unkissed."

The old woman clucked her tongue. "You should not make promises you cannot keep, especially as you make your pledge. The binding must remain intact until dawn, so there will be many things you cannot do with your bride this night."

Kael's brows drew together and he frowned at her darkly. "What can't we do?"

"You must avoid the wren," the witch added, "for that position would strain her shoulder too much. The centaur, too. And the wolf—"

"No," Kael said flatly. "I will have her that way."

"It cannot be done."

His fiery gaze caught Anja's again. "We will see about that."

The old woman gave him another warning look, which went unheeded. Clucking her tongue again, she lifted the two ends of the red ribbon, which had been wound through their fingers and around their wrists but was still untied.

In a raised voice, she announced to the now-silent crowd, "These two are not yet bound together. So we gather to witness their joining, as two become one."

Her heart thundering, Anja smiled happily up at Kael—who did not smile back, but watched her with all-consuming hunger smoldering in his eyes. His palm was like a hot stone against hers. His body seemed preternaturally still, as if simply waiting for this binding to finish before exploding into motion.

With a quick glance at Anja, the witch said, "Princess Anja of Ivermere, do you—"

"Anja the Wolfkiller," Kael added. "And the Huntress."

She began again. "Princess Anja of Ivermere, the Wolfkiller, the Huntress, do you pledge yourself to this man and vow to be his faithful wife?"

"Yes," she said breathlessly.

"Wife," Kael echoed on a growl, then threw his head back and roared, "*Is that bedchamber ready?*"

From the corner of her vision, Anja saw the innkeeper and his wife turn deathly pale, then rush away.

"I don't care if it isn't," Kael said, his eyes hot on hers. "I will take you upon this floor if I must."

"You will not take her yet," the witch said. "We have first your pledge to finish, and you have names to last all night."

"Then begin saying them, woman!"

The witch took her time before starting, mumbling his names to herself and counting upon her fingers. Then she lifted her voice and said, "Kael of the Skull Clan of the Dead Lands, the Butcherer, the Pitiless, the Conqueror, the Raviner, *also* the Wolfkiller, but only a small wolf, and with a rock—"

That was said with a sly smirk and twinkling eyes, but Kael gave no reaction, his gaze only for Anja. Only when she giggled did he respond with the barest twitch of his lips.

"—Disemboweler of Eathe, Silencer of Qul Wrac, Destroyer of Toatin Zan—"

A hearty cheer rose from those Kael had known from the mines.

"—Slaughterer of Geofry the Child-Eater—"

That drew a roar of approval from everyone, with clapping hands and stomping feet that was so loud and went on for so long that Kael bellowed for silence so she could continue.

"—Ruler of the Four Kingdoms of Grimhold, Vale, Lyngfen, and Dryloch." A frown creased her wrinkled forehead. "Is that all of them?"

"Kael the Free," Anja said. "That is the most important."

"No," he returned, his voice so guttural that each word seemed to emerge from deep within his broad chest, and his fingers shook against hers. "There is one more important that I do not have yet—Kael, Husband to Anja."

"Then do you pledge yourself to this woman?" the witch asked solemnly. "Do you vow to be her faithful husband?"

"I do," he said hoarsely, bringing their bound hands to his heart. "Forever."

The old woman tied the ends of the ribbon together.

"Then you are now wife and husband—"

It was Anja who moved first, leaping forward and catching his hair with her free hand and dragging him down for a kiss. Though there was not much dragging, for he met her halfway, capturing her parted lips beneath his own, then delving past them with a penetrating lick that pierced her to the hot, liquid core between her thighs. The villagers' cheers and stomping began again as Kael's mouth ravished hers. Then the villagers might as well have vanished, because he was her husband now, and kissing her as if she was his next breath, the next beat of his heart—and for the very first time in her life, Anja felt completely and deliciously wanted. And beyond that, *needed*.

With a rough groan, Kael locked his forearm behind the small of her back and lifted her up against his chest, their bound hands trapped between them. His mouth never relinquished hers as he strode through the crowd, each step bumping her knees against his thighs until she instinctively wrapped her legs around his hips.

And by the gods—how incredible it felt to have his rigid length between her legs instead of against her bottom. That had been thrilling, too, simply having him so close. But now with every step there was pressure against that spot he'd promised to lick, and she only had to rock her hips to increase the pressure, increase the friction, creating a wild storm of pleasure deep inside.

His mouth tore from hers as he began to the navigate

the stairs that would take them to their bed, and where he would give her all the things he'd said. With his mouth, with his tongue. Until he was deep inside her.

Inside her, inside her, inside her. Exactly where she needed him to be, to quiet this raging storm building within.

Panting, Anja wildly kissed his neck, his throat. "Hurry, Kael," she urged him faster. "I've waited so long already."

Not even knowing what she was waiting for. Pleasure, yes. But she'd never imagined something so frantic, so sweet as this.

His groan reverberated through his chest. "Then why did you not invite me to kiss you before this?"

"You sent me home," she reminded him, and through all the sweetness, a fresh pang struck her heart. Closing her eyes, she held him tighter, buried her face against his neck. "It is good you asked for forgiveness this Midwinter. So I'll forgive you for leaving me alone this eve, believing you'd rejected me again."

Abruptly he stopped, which was not what she'd intended for him to do. With their bound hands, he used the backs of his fingers to urge her chin up, for her eyes to meet his. Remorse carved sharp lines through his features. "I only wanted to bind you to me as quickly as I could."

"I realized…after," she said thickly.

Gently, his mouth brushed hers. "I will do better, wife."

It was already better. Tightening her fingers in his thick hair, she lifted against his erect length, deepening the kiss. But something had changed. Where he had been so impatient before, promising to take her on the floor if their bed wasn't ready and roaring at any delay, now his tongue leisurely stroked over hers as if there was no hurry at all.

Oh, but there *was*. Yet no matter how she moaned and rocked desperately against him, Kael kissed her in the same way that he walked—a steady prowl, as if he were searching out all the pleasure that could be found between her lips. But she *needed* his volatile burst of action, instead.

Yet even passing into the bedchamber didn't speed him. Slowly he lowered her to the bed. Slowly he came down over her, pinning their bound hands beside her head and bracing his weight upon his knees. When he broke the kiss, she whimpered and arched beneath him, yet he didn't push apart her thighs and shove his cock deep inside her as he'd promised.

Instead he started at the first promise, softly pressing his lips to her cheeks, her nose, her chin. Kissing every inch of her skin. Steadily prowling again.

She was far beyond that. "Kael," she begged. "Please."

His response was to tilt her chin back and kiss the length of her neck. Anja shivered with pleasure for every touch of his lips, yet still it wasn't enough. She used his own words, too desperate to even blush, hoping to prod him into that explosive rush. "I need you to fuck my… fuck my…"

Oh she could *not*.

"Virgin cunt?" His voice was a deep growl against her throat.

"Yes," she breathed.

He only kissed the hollow beneath her ear, then sucked on her lobe. She moaned and her fingers clenched in his hair as she felt that erotic pull through every womanly part of her. By the gods, her ear. How did that feel so *good*?

But not as good as the pinch of his teeth. She gasped, her entire body afire, and he said hotly into her ear, "You have another name that we did not use in the pledging: Anja the Virgin. And while you are still she, my wife, I will be Kael the Gentle and Slow."

She laughed breathlessly. "I just want you to be Kael the Thorough, and rend my maidenhead with your sword."

His amusement joined hers, and he shook against her. "I promise you I will do that."

"Oh, yes. Please," she sighed. "Please."

His smiling lips returned to hers again. "And the witch was right," he murmured. "I cannot kiss every inch tonight. With our hands tied together, we cannot even remove our tunics."

Anja stilled beneath him. It was true. They could remove their shirts partially, but not the sleeves on their bound arms. "I would suggest we tear it. But I have no other warm tunics. So what will we do?"

"We will do nothing." With sharp teeth, he nipped her bottom lip. "There is a reason why brides wear gowns."

Because it didn't matter if the gown could be removed, as long as it could be lifted. Now Anja shook as she felt the fingers of Kael's free hand journey up the length of her leggings from knee to upper thigh, then gently tug at the strap.

Eyes burning into hers, he rasped, "These have driven me mad, wife. Every day within the saddle. Knowing you were so bare. Your warm cunt so near to my cock. Every step the horse took, I dreamed of taking you."

Something inside her clenched tight. "I dreamed it, too," she whispered.

Her confession seemed to rip through him. He didn't move, but suddenly his muscles seemed coiled tighter, his face dark with hunger.

"Tell me what else you dreamed."

So much. But the one she could not stop imagining— "When you tended to my leg, I thought I might, I thought…" This needed courage, too, but she found it. "I thought I might grab your hair and force your mouth against my…virgin cunt."

She barely breathed the last. And she recognized the man before her now, had seen him splattered with blood and wielding an axe. No longer prowling.

His strong hand gripped her thigh and shoved it wide. Abruptly he moved down, pushing her tunic above her hips, baring her most intimate flesh. His eyes feasted hungrily upon the sight, and he drew in a deep breath. Ecstasy shined from his face when he filled himself with her scent. But he didn't kiss her there.

Instead he growled softly, "You are drenched in your sweet honey."

She knew it. Could feel it. So hot and wet and aching.

His beribboned fingers tightened on hers. He looked up at her face from his vantage between her spread and trembling thighs. Voice hoarse with need, he commanded, "Do not make me wait any longer, Anja."

She did not realize what he meant at first—then suddenly did, and was unsure until the moment she pushed her fingers into his thick hair. Everything within her shook with unbearable tension as she forced his head down to her mound.

Softly he kissed the white curls. Then his fingers exposed her sultry flesh and his broad tongue licked upward from her entrance, before circling the throbbing spot at the apex of her slit. Sheer ecstasy ripped across her nerves. She cried out, her fingers losing their grip in his hair, but he clearly needed no guidance or encouragement anyway.

His ravenous groan filled the chamber. "You taste even sweeter than I dreamed, Anja."

Hungrily he buried his face between her thighs and feasted, his tongue an unbearable torment and the most pleasurable heaven. But there was something more coming, she could feel it approaching, terrifying and exhilarating, but too much to bear, far too much. Yet when she tried to writhe away, Kael pinned her hips and sucked on that spot, the spot that would kill her, because she couldn't survive this. She begged, but he was relentless, and she screamed as it descended upon her and ripped her apart.

Then she was brought back to glorious, incredible life, where all the world was sharper and brighter and sweeter, with Kael kneeling between her thighs and softly kissing her mouth.

His head lifted, his gaze searching her flushed features. "You are well?"

Dazedly, she nodded.

"Then wrap your legs around me, Anja." His voice roughened. "You will feel pain this one time. Bite me if you must to stop your screams. Or if you wish to hurt me in return."

She didn't ever want to. No matter how much pain there was. And all of the torment and pleasure he'd given with his tongue had made her wetter, so much wetter, so the blunt pressure seemed not like pain when Kael's swollen manhood breached her entrance, but an almost unbearable stretching as he made a place for himself inside her.

Then a deeper place when he gritted out against her lips, "Your cunt is flooded with your hot welcome, yet it still fights me for every inch," before withdrawing and leaving behind a burning sting. Only a moment passed before he gripped her bottom in his big hand and pushed into her again, tilting her higher as he did, and instead of one long stroke he filled her in short, hard thrusts. Her fingers squeezed his ever tighter as she bore the endless intrusion. Tears leaked from her eyes though his invasion didn't hurt, it was just too full and too tight—and the pleasure she had hoped for was only found in his nearness and his warmth and the weight of him above her, in the soft press of his lips to the corner of her mouth, and in the blessed relief that he had apparently finished so quickly. Though his manhood was still swollen and enormous inside her, he didn't move now, but brushed her hair back from her face and wiped away her tears.

Shakily, she smiled at him. "It only hurts this one time?"

Expression taut, he gave a short nod.

She raised trembling fingers to his mouth. "Is this what you would have had me forgive? The thing you hadn't yet done?"

"No." His voice was gruff. "I intended to steal you from Ivermere tomorrow and take you back to my stronghold—whether you wished to or not."

"I would have wished to." Trying to ease the depth of the thickness still lodged within her, she unwound a leg from around his back and braced her foot upon the mattress. A tremor moved through Kael's big body, held straining and motionless above her. Did it take so long to finish? Or had he forgotten he was there? She could not forget. All she could feel was him, and the tight stretch of her sheath.

"You are still inside me," she reminded him gently.

He laughed and groaned at once, his head hanging down like a man at the end of his strength. "Are you still hurting?"

"No." But not enjoying it, either. "You are just…so deep."

Immediately Kael eased back, but not to withdraw. Instead his arm tightened around her and he drew her up with him, until he was sitting on the bed and she straddled his hips, face to face. They were both still fully dressed, though her tunic was pushed up to her waist and he had unlaced his breeches. Her leather-covered knees sank into the mattress. Her inner walls still felt so tight and full, but the deep discomfort was gone, because now she could rise higher on his manhood.

Curious, she glanced down and stilled, mouth parting as she saw his erection, only partially inside her now. He was fully swollen, the thick shaft glistening with her wetness and streaked with her virgin's blood—but no seed. There ought to be seed.

Her gaze flew to his. "You have not spent?"

His answer was a kiss, hot and deep and slow. Another followed, then another, and those were pure pleasure, as were the kisses he bestowed to her cheeks, her jaw, her throat.

He unlaced her heavy tunic and exposed more skin. Supporting her with his forearm, he eased her back slightly. The movement forced him deeper inside again, but even that was not so uncomfortable now—and obviously pleasurable for him. With a deep groan, he used his teeth to tug the open neck of her tunic down, revealing the pouting tip of her breast. He latched on, drawing hard upon her nipple. Gasping, Anja arched her back, the motion pushing him even deeper. But there was no discomfort. Only the sudden, taut clench of her inner muscles.

"Kael," she breathed, clutching at his shoulder. "Kael."

But he only continued sucking on the turgid peak of her breast, and she could not bear it, because he was so deep inside her yet she needed more. So much more.

Tentatively, she lifted her hips, was rewarded with the delicious slide of his erection within the tight clasp of her inner walls. Her breath shuddered at the unexpected pleasure, and she raised her hips again, a sharper movement that took him deeper.

"Oh," she whispered and saw Kael gazing at her with heavy-lidded hunger.

Using their bound hands, Kael slowly drew her upright over his lap again. In a voice taut with strain, he asked, "Are you ready for the rest?"

—*to fuck your virgin cunt and fill you with my seed*—

In answer, she fisted her hand in his hair and kissed him. For he had not only made a place for himself by pressing inside her—she had made a place for him, and she saw his pleasure and his torment while he was within her, and these gifts weren't just his to give to her, but hers to give to him. So she did, rising up and loving his deep groan. Sinking down and feeling him shake in ecstasy. Then shaking, too, when he pushed their bound hands between them, and began stroking his fingers over that terrible, wonderful spot. Slick with her arousal, their fingers teased together, until she couldn't bear it anymore, couldn't stop riding him, or kissing him, and she cried out against his mouth when she shattered apart again.

With a savage growl, he shoved her over onto her back, his cock deep inside her, fucking her with fast, brutal strokes. She urged him on with her mouth, with her hips, with her fingers tightening on his—until he abruptly stilled, his eyes locked on hers.

And as she felt the deep, hot pulse of his release inside her, Kael the Conqueror didn't bellow or roar. Instead he breathed her name reverently, as if it were a prayer...or as if she was an answer to one.

9

KAEL THE FREE

Dryloch

ON MIDWINTER MORNING, KAEL'S BRIDE awakened him with a kiss. Then she whispered into his ear, "You were sleeping so soundly, I could have put a dagger to your throat."

Without opening his eyes, he grinned and reached for her—not catching her bare limbs, but the sleeve of her tunic. Already dressed again?

Neither he nor his wife had slept that night, and the moment that dawn had arrived, he'd unbound the red ribbon, stripped Anja naked, and truly kissed every inch. Only afterward had they finally found their rest, though it could not be a long one. If they didn't leave by midmorning, then they couldn't reach Ivermere and return to the village without being caught in Scalewood when night fell—which meant delaying for another day. The wards kept the forest safe after dark, but it was harrowing enough when the sun was high, and Anja had already told him she preferred not to stay overnight in Ivermere.

Kael would have gladly stayed in bed here for another day. But he was even more eager to finish their journey to Ivermere and kill the cursed spider, so his bride would have no worries preying upon her mind. *Then* he would take her to bed for a week. Before they left, Kael would tell the innkeeper to keep the chamber ready for their return and a longer stay. They had no reason to rush the journey home. They could wait for the caravan with her trunks to arrive, and make use of the benches in the carriage all the way back to the stronghold.

It was a fine and wonderful thing, being king.

Easing open one eye, he judged the light in the room. Too bright for early winter morning. "Did we sleep too late?"

"Almost. But there is time enough for you to break your fast before we go." With her white hair braided into a pretty crown, she smiled down at him—and Kael had never seen such a beautiful sight in all his life. "Tarry in bed another moment, though, or else you will give the villagers an eyeful. They have asked to bring us a small Midwinter feast, since we will miss the midday feast in Ivermere."

"I would rather feast upon my wife."

A blush stained her cheeks, but there was promise and heat in her dark eyes when he brought her down for a lingering kiss…then reluctantly let her go.

The innkeeper had made up the adjoining chamber to be a parlor for them, and by the time Kael had relieved himself and dragged his breeches on, the villagers had come and gone. Their *small* feast had a trestle table groaning beneath its weight, and no doubt included the roasts and pies that the villagers had intended for their own Midwinter celebrations. Which meant that he would need to sample a small amount of everything on that table, so that no one was slighted by the king—or left with nothing.

Fortunately he had a strong appetite, and a wife with an appetite of her own. With a laughing smile, she gestured to one end of the table.

"I can manage these dishes," she said, tossing to him a pewter spoon. "But you will have to see to the remainder."

It would be no challenge at all. A flavorful roast was first, then a bite of pork pie, then a sausage with crackling. He glanced up at Anja when she made a soft exclamation, her mouth stuffed with a pear tart. Her widened eyes met his, but as he could see the laughter in them, so he continued on to a slice of venison until she could speak.

"I have just remembered that my mother asked me to bring winter pears back from one of my rides," she said while dipping her spoon into a cherry pudding. She had taken the end of the table that held the sweets, he suddenly realized, and felt a swell of pride at his wife's cunning. "She doesn't like pears for herself, but they are common Midwinter gifts and we were nearing that season, so I thought nothing of it since. But it was later the same day when she and my father told me that your letter had arrived. So they had already intended to send me to you as a bride, because she planned to give me the kissing potion even then—so that I could be sent away without any resistance. They must have been astonished that I agreed so easily, instead!"

She was laughing but Kael couldn't join in. Just mention of that potion darkened his mood—and he didn't follow the rest. "What do pears have to do with it?"

"Winter pear seeds are part of the potion, and it's more effective if they are gathered by the person whom the potion is intended for. Otherwise the potion will only last a few days. But if tailored to one person…weeks. Months, if the body is cared for properly. They can only be awakened with another sip of the potion." Suddenly her amusement faded. Her face clouded, and she pressed her bottom lip between her teeth before turning to cut free a piece of cake. "But they didn't need to use it after I agreed to go. Not until I saw the spider a day or two later. Then they believed I'd changed my mind, yet sent me anyway."

Into the arms of a man that everyone believed would be cruel to her. "Did they know you intended to kill me and take my throne?"

Silently she shook her head.

He contained the rage boiling through his veins. "You never need to see them again. I will continue to Ivermere today and kill the spider. Or not, if you wish us to be done with them completely."

"I am already here," she said in a quiet voice, and resolutely dipped her spoon into another pudding. "I will see it finished."

He could not bear her hurt. Swiftly he strode around the table and caught her chin, tilting her face up to claim a kiss. Warm honey and tart cherry flavored her lips, and she softly sighed and melted against him.

When he lifted his head, there was still a touch of melancholy and pain in her smile, but also steely resolution. "After today, I will not think of them again," she said.

She would not be able to help it, but Kael would do his best to keep her distracted, so she would not think of them too often. He swiftly kissed her again, then looked over the sweet dishes, looking for apple pastries to take back to his end of the table.

Her spoon digging into a nearby bowl, Anja made a small sound of surprise. He glanced at her and found her tilting her head, to better see the faintly glowing rune etched into his side. With her fingers she traced the shape that curved along his ribs, her brow furrowing.

Her puzzled gaze lifted to his. "Why is a ward marked into your skin?"

"To protect me from sorcerers' spells." He could not have defeated any of Geofry's warlords without it. They'd have burst his eyes or broken his neck with a few words. But the ward made him impervious to their magic.

Not impervious to other things affected by their magic, though. If they had cast a spell to fill a room with water and locked the doors, Kael might have drowned. But in all cases, Kael had destroyed them before they'd figured out that they needed to kill him with indirect spells.

"Yes, but…in your *skin*? And it's active and glowing," she said in wonder. "Does your Minister of Wards do this for you? Where did he hear of such a thing? Not in Ivermere. And how did he maintain its power in the two weeks since you left the stronghold? It should have faded within days."

Should have. Except it was nothing like she assumed. And suddenly Kael realized that, of all people, Anja might be most hurt by the truth of this. Because he had never lied to her. But she had believed *he* would be angry when he discovered the truth about her magic. She'd thought such omissions of truth were something to be angry about. Now it was the same situation…but reversed.

With tension gripping his throat, Kael shook his head. "I made it."

She fell silent. For the longest moments of his life, she simply regarded him with solemn, dark eyes.

When she spoke, her tone was flat. "You are a spellcaster?"

"No." He knew no spells, and wouldn't have used them

if he did. "But I was born in the Dead Lands—and the Reckoning did not destroy the ability to use corrupt magic, only everything that had been changed by it before. So my people are still born with the ability, just as everyone in Ivermere is. But aside from the witches and a few healers, none use corrupted magics. And there is this."

He showed her the small mark at the inside of his elbow. As if he'd shown her a crawler, Anja gasped in horror and fell back a step. Her hand flew to her lips and her eyes shot to his, outrage and astonishment combining into— "Who did that to you?"

She looked as if she might strike down the culprit with her sword. She would not have to go far.

"I did." Because it bound his magic to his skin. He could not even inadvertently cast a spell, because he couldn't draw on anything from outside himself, stealing it from elsewhere. His natural ability could power the ward embedded in his skin, but that was only a shield that prevented corrupted magics from touching him, not a spell that stole safety from one place and gave it to another.

His answer had not lessened her horror. "In Ivermere," she said, "this is the worst punishment. A mark of shame, even worse than death."

Did she think he had been punished? "And in the Dead Lands, it is a choice." Because she was still shaking her head, with tears standing in her eyes, he added, "There's no shame in it. Instead it declares the kind of man I choose to be. If I harm anyone, it will be because

I *mean* to harm them, not because a spell has scaled and stolen something from someone else."

Drawing in a shuddering breath, she finally nodded, as if accepting that view of it. She smoothed her fingers over the small mark—as if she meant to comfort him, to ease his pain, though there was no pain to ease.

No pain that was *his*. Because her voice was thick as she told him, "It's not chosen in Ivermere. It's a punishment given to criminals. It means exclusion and exile from the realm. And if you delay in going, they will hunt you down and cast you out."

Ragged emotion opened a hole in his chest as understanding speared through him. In many ways, she had been wearing that mark all of her life, though invisibly. A mark that was a punishment, a mark of shame.

And she had said so many times that she was her parents' shame. As if her inability to cast spells was a punishment. Then this very morning, she'd realized that her king and queen had essentially cast her out.

He'd understood that she'd been hurt. But he hadn't understood how deep the hurt must have gone…or how deeply he must have hurt her last night, too. When she'd asked for a kiss, everything Kael wanted was suddenly placed in his hands, and he'd rushed to secure it before she slipped away. Yet to Anja, it must have seemed another part of her lifelong pain. She had once again been unwanted, rejected. Cast away.

Never again would he allow her to feel that way.

Catching her face in his hands, he looked into her eyes. "You are not a punishment, my Anja. You are the greatest gift."

Her lips parted in surprise, her brow furrowing. She stared at him with a chaotic storm of emotions sweeping across her face, chief among them confusion. As if she couldn't understand what he was saying—or *why* he would say it.

Then he would make certain she knew. "Never could I imagine a woman who has added so much light to my life. I was smothered and dying, and now every breath is free. When we return to Grimhold, no matter how many meetings I sit through, with you at my side every moment will be a joy."

He knew from last night what her happy tears looked like, and they were the same as the ones now shimmering in her eyes. In a trembling voice, she said, "We will still make certain there are not so many meetings."

If that was her response, then she didn't understand what he was trying to say. "I won't care if there are. Everything else might remain the same, but everything for me will be changed," he told her gruffly. "That is what loving you has done to me. It has changed everything."

She went still, her dark gaze searching his, her face alight with wonder and hope. "You love me?"

"I do." His voice deepened. "I know you do not yet feel the same, but I will win your heart—"

"I do! I do feel the same." Those happy tears filled her

eyes again. "Did I not tell you last night?"

Anja loved him. *Him.* The Conqueror, the Butcherer, the Raviner. He had more blood on his hands than an ocean could wash away. Yet she loved him.

The emotions swelling and rising in his chest threatened to choke him. "You only said that you wanted me."

A blush stained her cheeks. "Maybe I was too distracted by the rest."

"Too distracted by a kiss to say you love me? You will have to do better than that, my wife." With his heart in his throat, he lowered his head and brushed his lips to hers. "Tell me."

Breathlessly she whispered, "I love you."

He kissed her throat and waited.

Hoarsely now, she said, "I love you."

He went to his knees. Her breath caught. Then her fingers slid into his hair as he lifted the hem of her tunic, revealing the sleek skin at the tops of her thighs, the soft tangle of white curls, the glistening pink flesh peeking out. "Now I will show you how a king eats his Midwinter feast."

She laughed, a sound lightened by amusement and roughened by her need. "By the gods, how I love you!"

And he could taste it, the sweetness of her love and need bursting across his tongue when he teased her with a single lick. She gasped another "I love you," her thighs trembling, the magic she possessed shining from her skin.

Powerful magic. It had to be. Because every one of his Midwinter wishes had come true. Anja the Kind would be at his side every day and in his bed every night. Anja the Courageous had pledged herself as his wife. And now Anja the Beloved had given her love in return.

And with every kiss, every lick, she would tell him again.

So Kael claimed her cunt and feasted like a king did—on his knees, to worship the queen who owned every part of his heart.

10

ANJA THE WITCH

Scalewood

IT WAS ALWAYS DARK IN Scalewood. The forest grew so tall and thick that the sun never touched the ground, except upon the narrow swath of road that passed from Dryloch to Ivermere. The path had been cut in ancient times, when the magic within the forest hadn't been so powerful and the creatures residing there not so dangerous.

If not for the wards placed at either side of the road, the forest would have consumed the path long ago. But every few paces stood a heavy column of granite marked with a rune, and the faint golden glow of the active wards were a constant, reassuring sight.

Yet still Anja's heart raced every time the thundering

steps of an unseen terror echoed through the trees. When limbs cracked and trees swayed beneath monstrous weights. When glowing eyes shone through the darkness and ravenous howls joined unearthly screams.

She clutched Kael's forearm as a giant creature emerged into the half-shadows beside the road, easily three times taller than their own height upon Kael's warhorse. Covered in shaggy fur the color of rust, it walked upright, yet there was no mistaking the monster for anything humanlike. A thick hump sat atop massive shoulders hunched over like an old man's. Beady black eyes peered down at them over a long and pointed snout lined with sharp yellow teeth and long, thick tusks. Overlong arms roped with muscle dangled at its sides. From one taloned hand dangled the remains of a half-eaten stag. The other held a bloodied club that dragged on the ground with every giant step, leaving a shallow furrow through the soft earth.

Though she felt his own tension, Kael softly kissed the side of her neck and said, "We are safe."

She knew. On a shuddering breath, she tore her gaze away from the hideous beast and focused on the path ahead. The thing kept pace with them, as they sometimes did with travelers on the road—but they rarely stepped fully out of the shadows. Some in Ivermere believed that the sun burned them, but Anja thought it more likely that they simply weren't stupid. The wards had been up for far longer than living memory, so any creature within this forest knew the futility of trying to attack humans passing through. And when the Mistress of the Hunt and her hunters rode this path, from the safety of the road they would use spears and arrows to kill any creatures that strayed near enough to target.

A shriek sounded from the western side of the forest. The beast screamed an answer, a ululating howl that rose to a painful pitch. Prancing uneasily, Kael's horse tossed his head, snorting.

With a soothing murmur, Anja leaned forward and patted its thick neck, then coughed and gagged as a putrid odor washed over them. She glanced over and wished she could unsee the sight of the beast defecating on a fallen tree.

Cursing, Kael nudged the horse into an easy canter. Anja began giggling as soon as she could draw a breath of fresh air, then fell abruptly silent when crashing footfalls sounded behind them—the monster catching up to them, then easily keeping pace with the running horse.

Kael slowed and the beast did, too.

She rubbed her palm over his tense forearm. "It will be well."

"Yes," he agreed. Then asked, "Are they known to throw anything at the road?"

"Are you worried about its club or what it left back there on the tree?"

His laugh rumbled against her back. "The club."

"Rarely. I think they know there would be no point to it. If it killed us, it couldn't come for our bodies to eat. And it would lose its club. It would be like throwing your sword into a river hoping to hit a fish. You might succeed, but you'll have neither fish nor sword at the end." She glanced toward the shadows again, saw something squirming beneath the fur covering the beast's hump, and quickly looked away again. "I can tell this place unsettles you."

Amusement deepened his voice. "Can you?"

"It is the first time your manhood isn't swollen behind me."

He gave a shout of laughter—but didn't deny it, she noted. Instead he lifted her hand to his mouth and pressed a kiss to her palm. "You are clever, my wife." A deep breath lifted his chest. "Are you angry?"

Frowning, she glanced back. "At what?"

"That I did not tell you about the ward, or the mark that binds the magic to my skin."

She shook her head. "Not angry. Afraid, at first—"

Hard fingers caught her chin, tipped her face up to meet the bleakness of his. "Afraid of me?"

"No. Only afraid that if you had magic, then you wouldn't want me. But only for a moment," she reassured him and watched the fire return to his gaze. "And that was not because of *you*. Just…what I expect from magic-wielders, because it is the reaction I have known from them all of my life. Then the feeling was gone." Burned away when he'd showed her the mark. "*Then* I was angry, but only because I thought you might have had the magic taken from you, and I was sickened to think that you might have been treated the way I have been. But now that I know you did it yourself, and why, I am only left with…awe."

He frowned. "Awe?"

"Wards are only as strong as the magic that maintains them. Yet Toatin Zan's spells didn't touch you, and he was by *far* the most powerful sorcerer in living memory. How long has it been since the Reckoning?"

"Countless generations."

"With each generation stronger than the last?" She laughed and settled against his chest again, her head resting back against his broad shoulder. "Yet so very few spellcasting now, and instead taught purer magics. I think the world should be glad of—"

Sour fear shot up through her throat like bile, choking her.

Immediately Kael held her tighter. "Anja?"

"The wards," she breathed, her terrified gaze on the nearest granite column. "They're not glowing."

The sudden tension in his arm squeezed the breath from her chest. As one, they both looked to the beast, but the creature had not seemed to notice any change. He walked through the shadows, gnawing on the stag's carcass, sharp teeth tearing into the flesh and ripping it free.

"It can't see the runes from that side of the column," Anja whispered. Yet that was hardly a relief. "But if it looks across the road, it might see that the western wards have failed, too."

"Perhaps not easily," Kael said. "The sun is bright. It can

be hard to see the runes glow when there is so much light."

"Yes." A violent shiver wracked her body, then another. "We are still an hour from the edge of the forest."

"It will be but twenty minutes," was his grim reply and nudged the horse toward a gallop.

"No no no." Her already-pounding heart racing faster, Anja caught his hand holding the reins. "Slow him again."

Kael pulled back on the reins, though she could feel the tremors that ran through his every muscle when he did, as if fighting to make himself to do it. She glanced over at the beast. It had increased its speed for a few strides but now matched walking their pace again.

"No running," she said. "If we run, it might not just be one monster's attention that we catch. And the others might be more observant. We need to keep riding at this slow pace—and not give it any reason to look this way more than it would otherwise. So don't draw your sword or ready your axe, as the sunlight shining on the metal might draw interest."

The faint grinding behind her could only be his teeth. A moment later he gritted, "I mislike this plan."

"I know," she said unhappily. "There is nothing of any of this to like."

His big hand tangled in her hair and he tugged her head back, kissing her hard upon the lips before releasing her.

"You *will* be safe," he swore.

Though cold sweat slithered down her spine, she nodded. "We will be."

She settled back again—not at ease, for that was impossible, but needing to have as much of Kael against her as she could. He pulled her in tight, his muscles like coiled steel springs.

"If more come," he said starkly, "We will not wait for them to see the wards are gone. I will take to the road on foot and draw them to me, while you ride for Ivermere at speed."

"No," she said, and lay her hand against his, just as they had been when woven together with the ribbon. "We are bound together."

His voice hoarsened. "Anja—"

"It will be well. We have powerful magic on our side."

He gave a harsh laugh. "We do, and it is called fear. It tells me to let you run—and perhaps will save your life, because no matter how kind or courageous you are, bones crunch the same between a monster's teeth. But I love you so desperately that I would fight all of Scalewood to keep you alive and to see you safely away. I love you so mightily, I might even survive it."

Tears stinging her eyes at the emotion in his voice, she shook her head. "I do not refer to fear or love or courage. I refer to knowledge. I am familiar with these woods, and I truly believe that we shall be unharmed if we continue at this pace, even if more creatures come near to the road. And if this one beast sees the wards are broken, better to fight him together."

"Knowledge isn't magic," he said flatly. "It is a tool.

Like a sword. Or medicine."

"Truly?" She pursed her lips. "I think it should be magic. Then what of trust? It seems as if it should be a powerful magic, particularly if shared between two people."

"It is."

"Then trust me, Kael," she said quietly. "Trust me now, and follow my lead. And if that beast crosses the wards, I will trust that you know how best to fight him, and follow your lead."

His lips brushed against her temple, a soft and swift kiss. He could not stop holding her and touching her, it seemed—and she felt the same, clinging to his hand, her fingers numb from the tightness of their grip.

From that point forward, every howl and crash from within the darkness of the forest seemed like a harbinger of their death. Horrible tension chained them for an endless minute when, on the eastern side of the forest, another giant creature emerged into the half-shadows beside the road, a stick-limbed demon with blue skin hanging from its skeletal frame in ragged sheets, bloodied claws as long as Kael's sword, and teeth like sharpened knives. But it only gave them one disinterest look before skittering back into the trees.

Finally she could see the tall granite pillars marking the entrance to Scalewood's passage, and the road stretching ahead through sunlight and snow-covered fields. It seemed those last few hundred paces took years to travel. Even after the humpbacked beast ambled back into the forest, she kept expecting every monster within the wood to realize the wards had disappeared and devour them.

Simply passing through the pillars did not make them safe—with the wards inactive, there was nowhere safe now—yet still it seemed a great weight slipped away. From Kael, too, as he began kissing the side of her neck, her face, then simply tangling his hand in her hair and pressing his hard jaw against her temple and holding her tight. And, for the first time since they'd entered Scalewood, his big shaft was swollen again.

"How did you know?" His voice was hoarse, as hers was, though they had spoken little in the hour. But her throat was so raw from the unceasing tension it seemed as if she'd spent that hour screaming.

"It's difficult to unlearn something that you've believed is true all your life. Especially if you don't have reason to look and see if it's *still* true. The monsters didn't have reason to look at the wards." A shuddering breath escaped her. "But we were also lucky."

He shook his head. "You are the only person to have ever ridden through Scalewood without the protection of the wards or spells and emerged alive. That was your courage and knowledge, not luck."

"You made it through, too."

"And without you to guide me, I would have been dead," he said. "It is I who am lucky, that I have such a wife. Do you know what a woman of great magic and wisdom is called in the Dead Lands?"

She did know. And her reaction to the word was some-thing she would have to unlearn, too. "A witch," Anja said.

"Yes. But I call this one my queen." His chest lifted against her on a deep, impatient breath. "How long must we ride at this slow pace?"

Because what lay ahead might be more terrifying than what lay behind them. The wards were not linked to any one magic-wielder's power, but to everyone in Ivermere. Replenishing the Scalewood wards was the single most important ritual of a spellcaster's day. Yet it must have been two or three days since anyone in Ivermere had done it.

"Until the crest of that hill, I think," she said. "We would not be easily seen from Scalewood past that point."

Then they would finally run. Because Kael was right. Fear *was* a powerful magic.

Hopefully it would help them reach Ivermere in time to save the people there—if there was still anyone left. And if there wasn't anyone to replenish the wards before all the creatures within Scalewood realized they were free, then all the world would soon know the same fear she and Kael had just lived through…beginning with the people in his four kingdoms. Beginning with the village where they had pledged their lives together and passed the night, where they had been given a fine meal from the villagers' own tables. But if the monsters escaped, their people would not spend the day celebrating a Midwinter feast.

They would *be* the feast.

KAEL THE CONQUEROR

Ivermere

BUILT BY SPELLCASTERS WHO REVERED balance, Ivermere was often called the most beautiful of all kingdoms, but Kael misliked the sight of it. Despite the kingdom's abundance and bounty, to him it seemed a cold and barren place, for he had never known life to be contained within symmetrical lines and perfect curves. Life as he knew it was coarse and unfinished, full of sharp edges and unexpected beauty, and so he could see little of it within this place.

But now he truly saw no life. Ahead lay the gate of the city. It was Midwinter's Day, yet no one passed through it.

He dismounted and reached up for Anja, whose pale

face and wide eyes were like knives across his heart. So much fear she'd known today. And it was not done yet.

Steam rose from the horse's sweat-lathered coat. The warhorse's sides bellowed, and he snorted great clouds of frozen air with each labored breath.

Kael gave the reins to Anja. "Stay here and walk with him until he cools. I will go ahead through the gate and look."

She tore her frightened gaze from the city ahead. "You don't see already?"

"I see that no one comes through the gate, and that it is oddly quiet," he said.

Her breath trembled. "Then you don't see the webs that stretch between the palace spires?"

Unease skittered down his neck. He saw nothing of the sort. Only stillness.

He shook his head.

Her lips quivered and her throat worked as she stared at him. In a strained voice, she said, "But…you *do* believe that I see it?"

Because no one else had. Instead they had ignored her warnings and sent her away.

"I believe in many things I cannot see, Anja. I believe anything you tell me." And he had meant to make her stay outside the city gates, where she might be safe from whatever waited within, but clearly he needed her with him. "So let us go ahead."

Drawing his sword, he waited until she'd drawn her

own. Though he'd rather have held her against him, better to have both hands free. Quietly he approached the gate, Anja a silent shadow in wolfskin behind him.

"Careful," she whispered and slashed her blade through the air. He could not see the strands of webbing that she cut, but felt the eerie brush against his tunic's sleeve as they fell.

"Did it cling to your sword?"

She shook her head.

"I have heard that spiders make different silks. Some like glue. Some not. So take care and try not to touch them." His eyes would not serve him as they should, so he listened at the gate for any movement within. There was nothing but the whisper of a breeze through Anja's hair and ruffling the hem of his fur cloak.

He tossed it from his shoulders and continued through. Behind him, Anja softly gasped in horror at the scene ahead—though he could not be certain what *she* was seeing. To him, it was clear enough. Men lay motionless upon the ground, all of them strangely rigid with arms tightly against their sides and legs together.

"Is that Lord Eafen and the soldiers?"

It was. By reports from the village in Dryloch, Lord Eafen had been a day ahead of Kael and Anja. So yesterday they'd passed through Scalewood while the wards were still intact. But it appeared as if they had been almost immediately ambushed after entering the city gates.

Grimly Kael moved forward to examine the bodies—and

found a soldier staring back at him, eyes wide open. The frightened depths pleaded with Kael for help.

Kael didn't know how to help him. "Anja?"

She was bending over another. "They're wrapped up in the webbing. Maybe I can—"

"Don't touch it!" he said sharply when she reached for the soldier's face, as if to tear the silk covering it away. "Not with bare skin."

She jerked her fingers away, then drew a dagger with a shaking hand. "What do you think it is?"

"A spell," he said grimly. "They are not simply wrapped in webbing. They are ensorcelled. This one cannot speak or fight against what binds him."

And Anja was not impervious to spells. Kael, however—

He dragged his fingers down the soldier's face, felt the resistance as the invisible webbing stretched, then ripped. When the man's head was free, he looked for any other exposed skin, and ripped the webbing from the soldier's hands.

A great shudder wracked the soldier's body. He began to struggle, wriggling like a fish.

"He's still wrapped in it," Anja said. She was kneeling and still carefully cutting the webbing from the other soldier.

This would take too long to free them all. Kael grabbed the soldier's shoulder to stop his flailing. "Be still!" he ordered. "And speak the words to replenish the Scale-wood wards."

One soldier's magic would not create wards strong enough to hold even one creature, but the glow would return. The beasts of Scalewood would surely attempt to break free if they saw the runes were dark…but if even one magic-wielder powered the runes, they would have to test the boundary to know that it was so weak.

The soldier babbled a few words and Kael looked to Anja, whose relief shone from her eyes.

But this would not be enough. "We cannot free these others now. If everyone in the kingdom is bound in the same spell, it would take an eternity for the two of us to tear the webbing from each." Because no one else could help do it. Anja was the only one to see the webbing. Anyone else who tried to walk through these streets and homes searching for others to free would surely only be caught and ensorcelled again. "But they will all be free if the spider is slain."

Lips pressed tight, she nodded. She hated leaving these men here as much as Kael did. But the remedy here was clear, and the same purpose they'd had since the beginning—to kill the spider.

"We will return for you," he vowed to the soldier, who was not much comforted by it, but that could not be helped. He stood from his crouch and looked to the others. Dread filled his chest. They were not all ensorcelled.

Lord Eafen was dead. A withered husk remained within his fine embroidered clothes, as if he'd been drained dry—and the puncture wounds in his torso could not have come from a spider the size of a cat.

"What is it?" Anja had stopped beside him, her gaze searching his face, then turning to look in the direction he was. "Do you hear something approach?"

She could not see the husk, he realized. The webbing wrapping the body concealed the damage from her eyes.

"It is Lord Eafen," he said grimly. "He's dead."

Her lips parted in dismay, then firmed. "I will lead the way. It will not still be in my mother's bedchamber, but we can start—"

She broke off, eyes widening and her gaze shooting higher. Muscles coiled, Kael spun to face the same direction…saw nothing.

"Anja?"

A wheezing breath left her, and she stepped back, her gaze still fixed ahead. "We need to run."

"What?" Again he searched the empty city ahead. "Why?"

She made a low, moaning sound of sheer terror. "It is not the size of a cat. Or a horse. It is bigger than…"

Words failed her. But it didn't matter.

"We can't run," he told her. "That soldier's magic will not hold Scalewood. And it is eating them. Lord Eafen, already. Probably others. Perhaps children."

Tears filling her eyes, she still didn't look away from the horror that held her motionless. "You can't be healed," she whispered. "You are warded against spells, so if you are hurt—"

"I will heal slowly." As he'd done before.

She shook her head. "I am the only one who can see it. I *will* find a way to kill it. And I can be healed. You should run."

Run? Leave her to face this alone? Stifling a shout of laughter, Kael grabbed the edges of her wolfskin coat and pulled her close. Startled, she tore her gaze from the spider to meet his.

"We're bound together," he reminded her softly. "Now *you* will trust *me*."

Though her breath shuddered through her pale lips, she nodded.

"How near is it?"

Her gaze darted past him. "Five hundred paces."

Still a fair distance away. "On the ground or above?"

"The ground." Her gaze flickered, and Kael saw the courage and cleverness he knew so well return like a light to her eyes, which narrowed. "I think it's too big to easily crawl on the walls and roofs."

Which didn't mean that it *couldn't*—but that it might prefer the ground, as it offered more stable footing. If retreating, it might flee upwards. But if defending against an attack, would likely remain in the environment where it had the advantage of familiarity.

That suited Kael. In a battle, he preferred the ground, too. "What weaknesses do you see?"

"The eyes. There are eight, and all at the front."

So it could be approached from behind. He nodded and waited for more.

She shook her head. "That is all."

That was never all. "What is the skin?"

"It looks as hard as armor."

Even armor would split beneath the blade of an axe. "When you chased the wolf whose skin you wear, you had spelled arrows that never missed their mark. Do you still?"

Hope lit her face. "In the hunters' armory. Its eyes—"

"You can blind it from a distance," he agreed. "And I will finish it."

She grinned and pulled him down for a quick, hard kiss before turning toward an alley. "Follow me."

They moved swiftly across the city, keeping to the narrow alleys that the spider couldn't follow them into, with unease scraping the back of his neck with every step. Frequently Anja's sword swept through invisible strands in their path, and his unease dug deeper each time she did, until it wrapped around the length of his spine with a cold, clawed hand. If the spider didn't move along the webs, why weave so many strands through the city? Why weren't the strands covered in glue to trap them like flies until the spider arrived to eat them?

Sudden realization stopped him in his tracks. "Anja!"

At the opposite end of the alley, she glanced back— then up, but even before her cry of warning rang out, he swung about and hurled the axe upward, roaring with the effort. The sharp *crack* as his blade bit deep was like the sweetest music, the sight of his axe embedded in the air itself a triumphant one.

A substance warm and sticky splattered his face. Anja screamed and he whipped around to see her charge toward him with sword at ready—then falter slightly, her head tipping back. In the air above the alley, his axe floated toward her.

"Run for the nearest open square and wait at the center!" he bellowed at her. "I will be right behind."

She hesitated, her frantic gaze moving over his face. "The web—"

"Was spelled." And the spider probably believed him paralyzed now, no doubt intended to return to wrap him up after it did the same to Anja. "Run!"

She fled.

Grimly he watched his axe as the spider continued after her. She would be slicing through any web strands in her path...and that would lead the creature straight to her. But with the path already cleared, and with no strands to break, Kael could follow without alerting the spider to his presence.

His blood thundering, he started after her. His bride raced ahead, clever and strong, but unprotected, and his heart could hardly bear the moments she was out of his sight.

Never did he allow the axe to leave his sight. He still could not determine the size of the spider, but by the shiver of marble and the faint dusting of snow that fell from the roofs as it crawled along their tops, the span of its legs was at least fifty paces. The belly—where Kael assumed his axe was embedded—seemed to skim just above the roofs, and so would be low and well-protected on the ground. How tall the back was, Kael couldn't know.

Ahead, the alley opened into a marble courtyard where Anja stood, her back against a stone statue at the center of a fountain, watching the monster's approach with a terrified face almost as white as her hair. Kael wiped his hands down his cheeks, coating his palms in the sticky substance. Then he took a running start at the side of a building, and launched himself at the wall. His powerful grip assisted by the gluey strands covering his palms, he began climbing, hauling himself up the sheer face of the building.

At the top, he sprinted along the roof's edge toward the square. His axe was skimming down the side of a building toward the ground. Kael drew his sword and adjusted the grip in his sticky hands. He would not be letting this blade go until this was done.

With a mighty roar, he sprang from the roof with sword raised high, gaze fixed on the axe below.

He didn't fall far, only a body's length before slamming into a hardened surface, his muscles absorbing the impact as he landed and dropped into a crouch. With all his strength, he drove the point of his blade straight downward, into the rounded back of the monster. The fragrance of cinnamon and cloves belched into his face. An unseen gush of warm, thick liquid coated his hands, but the glue on his palms prevented the sword from slipping in his grip. Gritting his teeth, he yanked the sword free and stabbed the creature again. But still the axe below him moved steadily toward the center of the courtyard.

The same direction that the head would be in.

Grunting with each thrust of his blade, he steadily made his way forward, a red haze of violence and rage dropping over his vision, until all he could see was Anja, still standing unharmed by the statue—and by the gods, he was going to make certain she *stayed* unharmed. The spider's armor became slick with the viscous gore, his boots slipping, but soon he was not standing on the armor but was knee-deep in the carnage, his own sweat dripping onto the spider's unseen body like rain falling on glass.

The haze lifted with Anja was shouting his name, and he glance up to see her pointing to a spot just ahead. He waded forward through the invisible pulpy mess he'd made, and when he saw her nod, drove his sword downward. Instantly the surface beneath him lurched, but he grimly held on, twisting the sword, digging it deeper.

Slowly, as if he were standing upon a leaf floating on the wind, the spider swayed and sank to the ground, carrying him down with it. When it came to a rest, he was still two body lengths above the courtyard's marble pavers. He wrenched his sword free and looked to Anja, who stared at him wide eyes, her hands cupped over her mouth.

Chest heaving, he asked her, "Do you think it is defeated?"

Wordlessly she nodded.

But he shook his head. "But not yet dead. There is a spell that still disguises it. I need my axe."

Dropping to the ground, he headed for the belly and wrenched the heavy weapon free. Then he returned to Anja and said, "Point me at the head."

When she did, Kael strode forward and began hacking, working his way deeper with each powerful blow, and began to believe the spider was not the source of the disguising spell at all when abruptly he was surrounded by a cavern of dripping gore. With a triumphant shout, he gave the cursed thing one more whack, then emerged from the head and strode straight for Anja.

With a broad grin, he told her, "It is done."

She nodded, her gaze sweeping the buildings around them. "The webs are gone."

Because they were spells, not webs, and so they'd vanished with the spider's death. Fortunate, because it meant they wouldn't have to cut free each person in Ivermere. Even now, they should be stirring free of the magic that had bound them. So Anja's and his work here was finished.

Gaze fixed on her lips, Kael stalked forward.

She backed up.

His grin widened. "Will you not kiss your king?"

A choking laugh burst from her. "I love you, but... No."

Laughing, he strode to the fountain—where his reflection was a dripping red mask with white teeth. Without hesitation, he dove into the waist-high water. Shocking cold enveloped him, but it was a sweet agony on his overheated and sweating skin. He emerged and scraped his hair back from his eyes. For the first time, he saw the full size of the spider laid out before him.

What was left of it.

Sitting on the edge of the fountain, Anja observed, "You were thorough."

So he had been. He stripped off his soaked tunic, his chainmail, and flung them to the marble pavers in a slop of wet fabric and the ring of metal. His fingers yanked at the laces holding his breeches up, and he had to thank the freezing water for dousing the hot steel he'd sported since Anja had pointed him toward the spider's head. For already he heard the city stirring, heard the confused shouts and running steps, and they would not be alone for long.

He stripped the leather breeches down his legs, then saw the shy glance Anja gave his cock from beneath her lashes. Even freezing water could not overpower the innocent eroticism of that look. Naked, he scrubbed the gore from his skin, and with his eyes invited her in.

Laughing, she shook her head. "If it were summer, perhaps."

"In the Dead Lands, this *is* summer."

She scoffed. "And you lived there only five years!"

"In the Dead Lands, five years is an eternity." While she laughed again, he slid his hand beneath the surface of the water and leisurely began to stroke his cock. She fell silent, biting her lip, her gaze glued to the pumping of his fist. "Your cunt is hot enough to warm us both, my wife."

Her face colored prettily. Unable to resist, he caught her chin and claimed a kiss, her lips like a fire beneath his. She leaned into him, bracing her hand against his chest, her fingers a burning brand upon his icy skin. With a lick, he tasted the sweetness of her mouth, and her soft moan in response lay her arousal as naked as his. Satisfied for the moment, he drew back. Her eyes were closed, her cheeks flushed.

Then, with a heavy sigh, she turned her head and cast her gaze up to the palace spires. "I suppose I should go and find out if my parents survived."

"No." His hard reply brought her gaze swinging back to his. "You are Anja, Queen of the Four Kingdoms. You do not go to them. They come to you."

Her brows arched. She tilted her head, studying his face. Then she shrugged. "Very well. Though they probably won't bother to come."

If they did not, this spider would not be the last thing Kael destroyed today. Bracing his hand on the edge of the fountain, he surged from the pool in a cascade of bloodied water, then caught a glimpse of purple from the corner of his eye. At the edge of the courtyard, a tall man gaped at the massacred spider.

"You there!" Kael called. "Send word to the palace! It is Midwinter's Day and the Scalewood wards have failed. The call throughout the city for the replenishing ritual must be made *now*."

Now the man gaped at him.

"Also tell your king and queen that Queen Anja awaits them here, upon her throne."

The man gaped at Anja.

"And I left a black horse and cloak near the city gate. See they are brought to me."

The man gaped at Kael's cock.

"Run!" Kael bellowed. "Or the next sword you see will be the blade that felled the Child-Eater!"

The man fled.

Bemused, Anja asked, "My throne?"

"Anywhere you sit will be your throne." He swept up his bloodied sword and the wet tunic, began cleaning his blade. "I pray my cock will be your favorite."

Her giggle left a smile that lasted only a few moments, and her gaze rose to the spires again. Kael forced himself to patience, for a king and queen just released from an ensorcellment that had taken over their realm could not immediately attend to anyone without first knowing what damage had been done. As there had been, judging by the grieving wails that found their way to the courtyard. Anja closed her eyes at each one, as if she felt that grief, too. But there was more than grief that he saw rising beneath her skin. Rage. It filled her as rage had once filled him, and he thought that the king and queen of Ivermere would be very smart to come before the fire of it built too much higher in their daughter.

The courtyard had filled with gawkers. Some ventured

close to Anja and Kael, and he gladly shared the tale of how Anja had demanded Kael the Conqueror's help at the point of her sword and insisted upon returning to Ivermere to slay the spider. How Anja had fought and defeated the bandit who'd tried to stop her from her quest. How Anja had boldly won the Butcherer's heart and had been named Queen of the Four Kingdoms upon Midwinter's Eve. How Anja had bravely guided him through the wardless forest. How Anja had been the only person with clear eyes to see the horror that had lain waste to Ivermere, how she had pointed him toward the killing blow. By the time he had told it several times over, the tall man in purple finally returned with his horse, his cloak, and a blanket.

Kael tied the blanket around his waist, though he was still too overheated for a cloak. He looked to Anja and decided they had waited long enough. He reached for his sword and axe.

A clatter of hooves drew his gaze. A procession of riders wearing gray wolfskin coats followed a golden carriage.

At his side, Anja gracefully rose to her feet. Blood streaked her cheek. Her braids had come partially undone, strands falling in a loose array around her face. The grime of two weeks of travel had collected on her boots and the hem of her coat. From the first time he'd seen her to now, there had been a hardening within her, like steel heated and cooled and tested. Yet she also burned brighter, so much brighter.

Her mother alighted from the carriage in golden crown and sleek gown. She wrinkled a delicately thin nose at the spider, then turned rounded eyes on Anja. The smile she had pasted onto her spell-reddened lips faltered.

Because she could not help but see what Kael did. What anyone with eyes must see. Even disheveled and dirty, wearing only her white hair as a crown, Anja was many times greater the queen that her mother was.

And this only her first day.

Her father emerged from the carriage after the queen. With features similar to his wife's, he looked nothing like Anja. Neither of them did. He turned a broad smile on Kael, gaze flickering only briefly to his bare chest. "We heard the King of the Four Kingdoms had arrived and slayed a monster in our midst. That is a fine introduction. Welcome to Ivermere, your majesty."

Still holding his axe, Kael commanded flatly, "Welcome my queen first. It was she who demanded we travel here to kill this spider—and in doing so, saved *all* of our kingdoms."

The queen's smile returned in full and she looked in wonder at Anja. "*This* is the spider you spoke of before? I wonder how it passed through the wards—"

"It didn't, Mother," Anja said tightly. "It didn't come from Scalewood. You created it when you made the kissing potion."

Genuine disbelief crossed the queen's face. "That can't be—"

"It *is*. The spell you used to create the potion scaled, and it did *this* to a common spider. The potion was intended to make my body helpless in sleep. The spider's webs did the same but kept everyone in a nightmare of unmoving wakefulness. You tailored the potion to me, the magic was intended for me. And the spider's concealment was intended for everyone *but* me." Her voice hardened. "*You* have done this. Ivermere helpless. The wards gone. All the world at risk from the creatures in Scalewood. *Because of your potion.*"

"I…" Her mother swallowed. "I only meant well. And you and your husband"—her gaze flickered to Kael's glowering face; she paled with fear and looked away—"seem to be getting on well. The spider is dead, and the wards are replenished. All is well again. There is no need for this anger or this unguarded speech."

"All is well?" Openly seething, Anja stalked closer to the queen. "People are *dead*, Mother. Your potion killed them. Your decision not to believe me when I said a spider lurked in your bedchamber killed them. Drugging me with the potion and sending me away killed them. All of these choices you made, you killed them, simply because you wanted to cast me out in the manner most convenient for you and for Father. Do you not see this?"

Bewildered, hurt, angry, the queen's cheeks stained with color as she looked to her husband, who was sighing and shaking his head. She looked back at Anja. "The scaling corrupted the spider, Anja—and *it* killed them.

Do *you* not see that?"

Her mouth in a flat line, Anja simply regarded her for a long moment. Then she quietly turned to Kael and said, "Nothing I say will make a difference. Let us go."

He lifted her into the saddle, swung up behind her. A courtyard full of round-eyed, thin-nosed spellcasters stared back at them—some looking uncomfortable, others outraged, others ashamed.

His gaze settled on the king and queen, and he thought that only kindness could have brought Anja here, braving the Butcherer and bandits and Scalewood, simply in hopes of saving her mother. It must have been kindness, because surely there was nothing here to love. "I will tell you what else has been affected by the scaling of that spell. You have lost a daughter, whose worth you were blind to. I have won a wife, whose value is all I see. She wields powerful magic, pure magic, though she is only just beginning to know the extent of her power. You would do well to send some of your people to Grimhold to learn with her, and learn from her."

Her parents exchanged a weary glance. Her father said, "Forgive me, your majesty. Anja has an unguarded tongue. If she has lied to you and said—"

"Do *not* disparage my queen!" His thundering roar echoed through the courtyard. "I have told you what she is. And if I *ever* hear word that you do not speak of Anja with the respect she deserves, then all of Ivermere will soon afterward discover exactly why I am called Kael the Conqueror."

And that was all that needed to be said. Kael touched his heels to the warhorse's sides and pushed him into a quick pace out of the courtyard and onto one of the main streets, ready to see no more of Ivermere.

Just beyond the city gate, a rumble of hoof beats came up behind them. The hunters, in their gray wolfskins. A tall, wiry woman with gray-streaked hair drew up beside Kael's horse—though careful to remain at a position lower than his.

"Princess Anja," she said.

Kael growled, and the hunter hastily amended it.

"Queen Anja."

Her gaze wary, Anja leaned forward to regard the other woman. "Mistress."

"We are riding ahead to make certain that no monsters breached the wards, so you will have safe passage through Scalewood." The Mistress of the Hunt's steady gaze didn't waver as she added, "Would you like to ride with us again?"

Anja's lips trembled before firming. "Not this day. Perhaps in the spring, however, you can journey to Grimhold, and we can speak about training hunters there. Scalewood does not hold the only dangers to our peoples, and the Four Kingdoms might need a Mistress of the Hunt."

"I think it already has a fine candidate." The woman grinned. "Queen Anja, who passed through the Scalewood unharmed. You will be a legend." She glanced at

Kael, tipped her chin. "Your majesty."

He nodded in return, and taking the gesture for the dismissal it was, she whistled and the hunters rode forward, cheering for Anja the Unharmed as they galloped past.

Though she hadn't been completely unharmed. She had raged at her parents, but also been disappointed in their utter unwillingness to listen to her.

"You are well?" he asked her softly.

"Yes." There was a hitch in her breath, but he recognized her happy tears. "It is just…there is truly a place for me. Here with you. And in our kingdoms."

Emotion tightened his throat. "There is."

Reaching back, she angled her head for his kiss—then huffed out a laugh. "My coat is bunched between us."

"That is not your coat," he said against her neck.

Her giggle shook her sweetly against him. "Yes, it is. Lift me up. I will show you how a queen rides double."

The gentle demand shot fire through his blood. With his hands spanning her waist, he raised her straight up. Her coat fell between them, curtaining her from his sight.

"Now turn me to face you," she said huskily.

Slowly he lowered her back to his lap, her legs spreading wide to straddle him. She wrapped her arms around his neck, pulled in close.

"The blanket." It was a breathless command. "Untie it."

He ripped open the knot at his hip and his cock sprang up between them. With a soft groan, Anja reached down and gripped his length, fitting him to her sultry entrance.

Kael gritted his teeth against a shout as she pushed down, her luscious hot sheath clasping his shaft in the sweetest embrace.

"I've claimed my favorite throne," she panted against his lips. "Now ride."

He would always obey his queen. So after a kiss, Kael the Conqueror claimed his bride.

Epilogue

THE MIDWINTER BRIDE

Grimhold

HERE WE ARE AGAIN AT Kael the Conqueror's mountain stronghold. A year has passed, and on this day, another Midwinter has come around. Within the great hall, trestle tables are laden with roasted meats and sweet pastries, and benches are filled with celebrants from all corners of the four kingdoms. But the merry conversation between them abruptly falls silent when, from the dais, a great crash and clattering sounds as the king sweeps platters to the floor—then lifts his queen from her golden throne and seats her on the table before him.

A sigh rises from many of those who sup, for this has happened before: the king will roar for them all to begone, because he has a royal feast to eat. But this time, no roar comes. The king is silent, staring up at his wife's face in awe and adoration, his great palm flattened over her belly…which is very slightly rounder than it was the year before. And suddenly, everyone within the room understands.

The queen has just given the king his Midwinter gift.

But such a gift from a queen is not only for the king, but also for a kingdom—or even four kingdoms. Cheers fill the great hall, along with the knowing nods from the maids who had not had to clean the queen's monthly rags since the harvest moon, and from the ladies of the court who had whispered behind their hands about how many naps the queen was taking of late. And amidst the noise the king's eyes grow hotter and hotter, and he opens his mouth—but before he can roar for them all to begone, the queen leans forward and puts her soft lips against his ear, perhaps suggesting that, on this day, the guests might be allowed to finish their meals. Without a word he rises and sweeps her into his arms—and the last sound that is heard from the king and queen that eve is her merry laugh as he carries her from the hall.

After they depart, a toast is raised to the man sitting beside the king's giant wooden throne—a toast that is raised every night after the king and queen retire to sleep (every night they are not tossed out of the great hall, that is.) There, all of the representatives of the four kingdoms salute Lord Minam, the royal chamberlain, for the wisdom and courage of posting messages to every kingdom near and far, searching for a bride—for he had brought to them the perfect one.

None knew that, among them, supped another who had answered those missives. Desperation had given her courage, but her journey had gone astray, and she had arrived far too late—but thought it was for the best, because never could she imagine being loved by Kael as he so clearly loved his Anja. So tomorrow she would continue on, whilst she still had the courage to go, and eventually find magic of her own.

But that is a tale of anotherwhere and anotherwhen… and, sadly, this Midwinter tale must come to an end.

Want more barbarian fantasy romance?
Look for THE MIDSUMMER BRIDE in 2018!
...now turn the page to enjoy the bonus story

A beauty unchained...

For ten years Cora Walker has yearned to return
to Blackwood Manor...and to her childhood
companion, Gideon Blake. But her dream of
returning home soon becomes a nightmare—
and the fully grown, dangerously sexy Gideon is
nothing like the young man she'd loved before.

A beast unleashed...

Cursed by the monster that killed his family,
Gideon sacrificed his heart to protect Cora from
the beast that lurks beneath his skin. But when
she returns and the curse chains her to his side,
he only has two choices: to persuade her to
marry him though he has stolen her freedom...
or die to save her from the beast within.

CHAPTER 1

Cora

"A̲r̲e̲ ̲y̲o̲u̲ ̲s̲u̲r̲e̲ ̲a̲b̲o̲u̲t̲ ̲t̲h̲i̲s̲, luv?"

It's the first thing that the hired driver, George, has said since picking me up from my London hotel just before dawn, when the full moon still lingered just above the western horizon. Since then we've traveled almost two hundred miles north, but the silence between us over the course of those four hours was a comfortable one. I was too preoccupied for conversation, anyway—with nerves tumbling in my belly, my heart full of hope, and my imagination racing as I pictured how Blackwood Manor might have changed in the ten years I've been away.

But I never imagined *this*. George stopped the car in front of the manor's gatehouse—the house where I lived

the first fifteen years of my life. The stone structure strad-
dles the lane that leads to Blackwood Hall, and serves as
the entrance to the estate. While I was growing up, never
once were those wrought-iron gates closed. Instead they
were always open, inviting visitors to continue on toward
the great manor house that sits like a crown upon the
escarpment overlooking the woodlands and beautifully
tended grounds.

Yet now those gates are closed. The heavy rusted chain
looped between the wrought-iron bars looks as if it has
been there almost as long as I've been gone. A weathered
sign reading "No Trespassing" hangs from the gatehouse
arch. The gatehouse itself, traditionally the home of Blackwood Manor's groundskeeper, appears utterly abandoned.

And those grounds are no longer beautifully tended.
The overgrown lawn beyond the gate looks as if no one
has held the groundskeeper's position since my father
left—since he took me from Blackwood Manor, the only
home I'd ever known. The home I've been dreaming of
returning to for ten years.

But judging by the disrepair of the gatehouse and
estate grounds, that home looks as if it has been left to
rot. And instead of nerves in my belly and a heart full of
hope, now despair thickens sourly in my chest.

Why had I been brought here? When I was contacted
by the Blake family's solicitor two weeks ago, he said that
my father's former employers had learned of his recent
death and wished to discuss the repayment of a debt. As

far as I was aware, they hadn't owed my father anything, and the solicitor hadn't been forthcoming with details. All I could imagine was that a severance had gone unpaid when he'd left their employ and they intended to bestow it upon his only living relative. Whatever debt they owe, they apparently felt it needed to be paid in person, so they arranged for me to travel from the Seattle airport to London, then hired a driver to bring me here.

But *why*? Clearly the Blakes don't live here now. If anyone still resided at Blackwood Hall, then those gates would not have gone unopened and chained for as long as they appear to have been. There would be some sign of the staff coming and going, because an estate and house of this size simply cannot function without people to care for it.

Yet obviously no one has been, and seeing the neglect feels as if a razor is slicing away at my heart.

The driver softly clears his throat. "Would you like me to take you back to the village, then, and see you settled at the inn?"

I tear my gaze from the gatehouse's sagging roof and broken windows. *At the inn?* A flutter of panic quivers through the heavy despair.

The reason I never returned to Blackwood Manor before now is simply because I *couldn't*. Especially after my father's long illness. Even before that, however, money has been scarce for years.

And although the Blakes bought my plane ticket and

hired George to drive me here, those arrangements didn't include a return trip—or a stay at a village inn. I assumed that would all be taken care of after I arrived. Blackwood Hall doesn't lack for guest rooms…and, in truth, I'd hoped that I wouldn't have to make that return trip back to the States. I'd hoped that there might be a place for me here, and that I'd either find employment on the estate—

Or something *more*. Because the estate isn't the only thing I left behind.

It's not the only thing I've dreamed of returning to all these years.

Because there's always been Gideon.

Gideon Blake, with eyes as green as spring and with a devil's smile. Two years older than me, we grew up together on the estate, but he was never like a brother—and always a friend. Until he was *almost* more than a friend. But we never got further than a kiss and a promise.

Then my father left his position here and put half a world between me and Gideon.

Of course I knew that my return might mean nothing to Gideon, and that everything I've hoped for was just a silly girl's dream—I can hardly expect him to remember a promise of love he made ten years ago, as a boy of seventeen—yet the possibility of finding a job on the estate hadn't seemed so silly.

I never dreamed that no one would be here at all, though. So I can't stay. But I've also got nowhere else to go. There's nothing left for me in Washington and the little coastal town where my father and I lived, even if I could afford the plane ticket back.

But although there's nothing for me here, either, I'd like to stay just long enough to say good-bye to the place.

After that…well, I'll figure something out.

"There's no need to take me back to the village," I tell George. "I'll get out here and walk up to the big house."

"But the gate's locked," he points out.

"I have a key to the gatehouse, so I can go through that way." Which is a lie, but I *do* know a way to enter the estate. When uncertainty tightens his mouth, I reassure him, "They probably just forgot which day I was coming. I'll find someone up at the house."

Though clearly unhappy with my decision, George obligingly retrieves my big rolling suitcase from the trunk. Outside the car, I pull on my lightweight jacket to ward off the chill in the air. The breeze sweeping across the grounds has a dank odor clinging to it, instead of the fresh and clean scent that I recall from years ago.

"You sure you'll be all right, dragging that luggage up the lane?"

"It shouldn't be a problem." I extend the suitcase's handle. "It's not heavy, and the lane is paved. It should roll easily."

"All right, then. Now I'll be stopping at the pub in the village for a bite of lunch. I expect I'll be an hour or so before returning to London, so you ring my mobile if you change your mind, and I'll drive here to pick you up."

His kindness helps to ease my despair, renewing my

natural optimism and the hope that brought me here. Surely the situation can't be so very dire.

Warmly I thank him, then wait until his car is out of sight down the narrow country lane before walking in the other direction. A stone wall surrounds the estate's grounds, with access gates the size of a standard door installed at regular intervals around the perimeter. Even when I lived here, those particular gates were always locked, but that never stopped me—and Gideon—from using one of them before.

The gate on the east wall is missing one of the vertical wrought-iron bars. The narrow gap allowed us to slip through as children—though by the time he was seventeen, Gideon had almost grown too large to fit. The last time we'd attempted it, he'd had to fight his way through the gap.

My step falters. That last time had been the night of my fifteenth birthday. Ten years ago, minus almost one month. The night he'd first kissed me. The night that had ended with something—*something*, I still don't know what it was—chasing us back to the safety of the estate. Then Gideon had gotten stuck pushing through the gap, and I remember the absolute terror and racing of my heart as I desperately pulled on his arm, trying to help drag him through, all the while hearing the growling approach of *something* through the dark.

I'd…almost forgotten about that. Because in the days following that night, my entire world fell apart. The next morning, Gideon came down with a terrible fever that worried his parents so deeply they'd flown him to see a specialist in Switzerland. Soon we received word that his fever had broken and he was on the mend. But even before they returned to Blackwood Manor, my father resigned and we left for the States.

I suppose in that time since, I told myself that Gideon and I simply overreacted to whatever had been out there on that moonlit night. I told myself that the overwhelming fear had followed hot on the heels of the thrilling excitement of our first kiss—and that we'd probably been spooked by a wild pig, but adrenaline and hormones had blown every snuffling grunt we'd heard into those ravenous growls and that bloodcurdling howl. Even right afterward, we'd been laughing at our own fear. Gideon had been limping as we'd crossed the grounds, because between my pulling and his shoving his big body through the gap in the gate, he'd ripped open a deep scratch on his leg. Yet we'd been laughing, giddy with sheer relief, and already teasing each other about who had been the more frightened—with Gideon claiming that the monster had been right on him at the end, and he'd demonstrated the hot feel of its breath against the back of his neck by bending his head and opening his lips against my throat, gently biting the skin there. I've never forgotten *that*. I've rarely thought about the rest, though.

Yet approaching the access gate now, my heart is pounding with remembered terror. My gaze scans the woods edging the lane, my heels tapping out a quick rhythm on the asphalt in my hurry to reach the safety behind the wall.

I haven't grown much since I was fifteen. Turning sideways, I slip through the gap in the bars as easily as I did then.

But I can't get my rolling suitcase through. I struggle with it until I'm breathless, but the suitcase simply won't fit through the gap. Even if I unloaded the contents, the rigid frame still wouldn't pass through.

Just *lovely*.

But not a real problem. Despite the gray skies, no rain is expected today. And when I reach the manor house, there will either be someone there or there won't be. If it's the first, we can come and collect my suitcase. If it's the latter…well, then I'll be rolling that suitcase to the village. So perhaps it's easier to leave it here now instead of hauling it back and forth across the estate grounds—and there's little fear that it will be stolen, since hardly any traffic comes out this way.

Even if it was taken, the suitcase contains nothing of real value. I only own one thing that I couldn't bear to lose, and I wear that around my neck.

The thin gold chain and teardrop diamond pendant was a gift from Gideon on that same birthday. He'd fastened it around my throat moments before he kissed me—and moments after he told me that I'd only be wearing it until we were old enough for him to replace it with a ring, because I was meant to be his.

Sweet, I know. Young love always is. Except that moment

had been far more than sweet. Even as a boy, Gideon had been intense, driven. At seventeen, he'd been like a force of nature—and he never made promises lightly.

Not that I intended to hold him to that promise when I returned to Blackwood Manor. Yet there *was* something between us, an affinity and attraction so strong that I've never experienced anything like it, not even briefly, with anyone else.

I'd hoped to find that again.

That hope doesn't seem likely now, and as I start walking the gravel path leading through the woodlands and to the manor house, the thin chain of gold around my neck feels unusually substantial, almost *heavy*—as if reminding me of its presence, and of all the dreams and promises that will never be fulfilled.

A walk through these woods should have cheered me some. Unlike the gatehouse and the grounds, there's no need to carefully maintain the grove, so the neglect visible around the rest of the estate isn't so apparent here. And the cherry trees should have been bursting with blossoms, a sight beautiful enough to lift the heaviest spirits.

Yet bare branches greet me, instead. Not just the cherry—the horse chestnut and beech trees raise skeletal, naked limbs to the gray sky, as if this were the dead of winter instead of the first day of spring.

So instead of strolling leisurely along the path, appreciating the beauty around me, I find myself walking briskly with my gaze fixed ahead and with unease prickling the length of my spine. Aside from the sound of my steps, everything is silent.

Not even the birds are singing.

Oh, and why did I dress up for this trip? With the idea of asking for employment—and perhaps seeing Gideon again—I'd put extra effort into my appearance today, leaving my blonde hair loose. Instead I should have pulled it back and saved myself the trouble of dragging the long strands out of my eyes every time the breeze picks up. Beneath my windbreaker, I'm wearing a pretty white blouse over a swingy A-line skirt that flirts with my knees on every step. But those steps would be a lot quicker if I wasn't wearing heels. If I were in my usual sneakers and jeans, the dread nipping at the back of my neck would have sent me sprinting along this path as fast as I could.

Instead I reach the clearing where Gideon and I used to practice hitting a cricket ball and stop in my tracks, staring in horror at the scene ahead.

One of the red deer that graze this estate and the nearby park has been slaughtered. Not just slain, as if by a poacher—but completely eviscerated, and what little remains of the flesh is scored by long, ragged tears. Blood splatters the surrounding grasses and leaves, and pools beneath the carcass in a thick, muddy sludge.

Red, glistening blood. This kill is only hours old.

Frantically I scan the grove, searching for whatever did this. But *what* could do this? We're in the middle of England, not the wilds of Alaska. Yet the deer looks as if it was torn apart by a pack of wolves. There's nothing like that here.

But if the estate has been abandoned, perhaps a pack of feral dogs now roams the grounds unchecked.

So screw my heels. Kicking them off, I scoop up the shoes and take off at a run, abandoning the gravel path for the softer grass along the verge. I don't have many talents, but if there's one thing I can do, it's *run*. Fast, far. Every morning back at home, I took to the beach and went as far as I could. Ten years ago, it was to escape my father and his angry refusal to tell me *why* we'd left, *why* I was hardly ever allowed to leave the house—except for when I visited the beach. Then he got sick, and I ran simply so I could breathe. After he died, I ran because I had to go somewhere. No longer escaping, but searching—because I was no longer bound to the house or trapped by the fear he never explained. Yet still never finding anything.

Finally, though—I'm running *to* somewhere.

Judging by the exterior of Blackwood Hall alone, I'd never have known the residence was abandoned. The brickwork and windows are all intact, the grand Palladian facade with its columned portico untouched by neglect. It's an enormous residence, built by one of the Blakes' noble ancestors, with a central three-story block flanked by four separate wings, each one perfectly symmetrical and square. The austere design is relieved only by the towers that cap the corners of the central block, and the overall effect is an imposing, refined stability, as if the house might stand for a thousand years and still elegantly reign over this countryside.

I race up the stairs to the main entrance. From this vantage point, I can see across the great lawns, all the way down to the gatehouse. No pack of dogs is in sight, but I'm still not waiting outside. Not with the memory of that red, glistening blood still so fresh in my mind.

The doors aren't locked. The hinges squeak as I push through into the grand hall. Cold silence greets me, the soft slap of my every bare footstep echoing faintly against the alabaster decorating the walls and domed ceiling.

"Hello?" I call out.

No answer but the hollow echo of my voice.

This part of the house was rarely used, anyway. If there *is* anyone left—a housekeeper, perhaps—they would likely reside in the staff wing.

Quickly I head in that direction, passing through the narrow corridor that connects the central block to the southwest wing. Here the neglect begins to show. Cobwebs lurk in the corners. Dust blankets every surface. My feet are filthy with it, but the thought of putting on my heels— imagining the empty clapping echo of every step—seems more dreadful to me than dirty feet ever could be.

But there *is* another noise. A faint, metallic slithering. Trying to detect the source of the sound, I slow as I enter the kitchen, where every Saturday morning Mrs. Collins used to chase Gideon and me away from her freshly baked scones.

Then I pass a window and my heart plummets straight to the ground, two stories below, where the south garden should have been.

The garden is still there. But it's dead. Not overgrown with weeds. Not untended with wildflowers running rampant through the carefully planted beds. Simply...dead. Nothing but withered stumps remain of the shrubs and roses, nothing but broken twigs littering the bare earth.

Hot tears burn at the back of my throat. That garden was *mine*. Not that it belonged to me—everything here always belonged to the Blakes. Yet it was mine to tend, mine to care for, and had been since I was old enough to plant seedlings at my father's side.

And if ever there was a sign that the hope I'd clung to was a fool's hope, that garden must be it. I held on to the memories of this house for so long, spent ten years awaiting the moment I would return. Yet nothing here held on to *me*. The soil itself had taken what I'd left behind and destroyed it.

There's nothing for me here. And instead of sweet nostalgia, every memory is bringing nothing but pain.

Feral dogs or not, it's time to go.

Blinded by tears, I turn back the way I came   and feel a faint sliding touch at the back of my neck. Immediately I shudder and flinch, thinking of those cobwebs, trying to bat away whatever just crawled across my skin.

But it's only my necklace. The pendant must have gotten turned around. Except...

I can't twist it back into place. The fine chain is snug around the front of my throat—and snug around the back of my neck—but my fingers can't locate the diamond pendant at the end of the chain.

Forget the pendant, though. I can't locate the *end* of the chain. Instead I turn and stare in stunned incomprehension at the glittering line of gold that trails behind me—starting at my nape and continuing the length of the corridor, where it disappears from sight.

What the…?

Shaking my head in confusion and disbelief, I slide my fingertips over the fine links around my neck, searching for the clasp.

There's no clasp. Instead the seamless chain circles my throat like a collar, with a golden leash that leads back toward the grand hall.

I follow it, uneasily aware that there's no slack forming in the chain as I go. It should be trailing behind me in an ever-increasing loop, but instead all of the loose length is simply…disappearing. Or shrinking. It's not being taken up from the other end, because the chain ahead of me isn't being pulled in that direction. As if the chain is only as long as it needs to be, and that length is the distance between my neck and wherever the chain ends.

Which isn't in the great hall. The chain leads across the domed chamber, past the long gallery still decorated with marble statuary and great paintings, and into the corridor connecting to the southeast wing.

The family wing.

Heart thundering, I pass through the main parlor—and here, finally here, there is not just abandonment and neglect. Though the wing clearly *has* been neglected. But the dust has not lain undisturbed. Instead it's as if someone has lived here and cleaned the rooms haphazardly, though not with the dedication of a household staff.

Cleaned the rooms…and destroyed some of them. Stuffing spills out of slashed upholstery. Silk wallpaper hangs in ragged strips. Shattered mirrors reflect shards of my face—the broken glass cleaned from the floor but the frames still hanging on the walls.

And there's blood. None of it fresh, but in faint hand-prints along the walls, and faded splotches in the rugs. I don't immediately recognize what those rusted stains are, but as soon as I do, it seems that I can't *stop* seeing it. There's blood everywhere.

Yet it's all smudged, indistinct. As if someone *tried* to clean it.

The level of destruction increases the deeper into the wing I go. And unless the chain is anchored outside somewhere, there's not much farther *to* go. The only rooms remaining in this direction are the solarium…and Gideon's bedchamber.

His room is the least ravaged, but only because nothing remains except for his big four-poster bed—as if every other piece of furniture and the rugs had been utterly destroyed or discarded.

This is where the chain ends, wrapped around the leg at the head of Gideon's bed. White linen sheets cover the mattress—and they're clean, though rumpled and unmade, but I can't mistake the faint, rusted stains for anything except more blood that didn't come out in the wash.

Hands shaking, I fall to my knees and attempt to pull the chain free. But it's not wrapped around the thick wooden leg, I realize. Instead the fine links seem to pierce *through* the solid oak, the diamond teardrop hanging from the opposite side as if it had been pinned there. Desperately I pull, thinking that if I pull hard enough the diamond will pop off and the chain will slide free, yet there's no give at all, and the pressure of the thin gold links against my palm and fingers threatens to cut into my skin.

I need a glove—or something else to protect my hand.

With frantic purpose, I strip off my jacket and wrap the fabric around my palm before gripping the chain again and hauling back with all of my strength, bracing my feet against the wall and throwing my weight into it.

Nothing happens…though the chain *should* have snapped. It's a fine piece of jewelry but a gold necklace isn't that strong.

It also usually doesn't stretch the length of a manor house, then shrink to less than three feet long. Right now it extends from the bed frame to my neck with no slack in between.

This isn't real. This *can't* be real.

The realization is a reassuring one, easing my panic

and calming the racing beat of my heart.

This can't be real.

So I'm dreaming. I must have fallen asleep in the car and now I'm dreaming.

Okay. My ragged breathing slows. Okay.

I'm okay. Just having a dream filled with some *really* disturbing symbolism.

But it'll end when I wake up. Letting go of the chain, I rise to my feet and look around the room. Gideon's bedchamber has its own access to the solarium—which, when we were young, was his favorite room in the entire house. The door leading to that glass-walled chamber has been torn away; nothing remains but the twisted, broken hinges. Gray daylight spills through the doorway.

And I know this is only a dream—a nightmare—yet still my heart freezes when I hear the soft growl coming from that room. Still my body begins trembling when I see the hulking shadow of...*something* prowling toward Gideon's bedchamber.

Something. Or someone.

Pulse thudding in my throat, I drop into a crouch beside the big bed, caught in an agony of indecision. If I run for it, surely the noise of my pounding feet and the slithering chain would alert them. If I stay right here, remain very quiet, maybe whatever is in the solarium won't realize I'm hiding. Silence seems like my best option.

But oh my god I want to run.

Abruptly the growling stops, replaced by the sound of...

an inhalation? As if someone is taking a long, deep breath.

As if something is scenting the air.

And they are in this room. In this bedchamber. And coming closer.

Cold sweat drips down my spine. Every muscle in my body tenses, preparing to flee. Then I hear a footstep, then another, coming ever closer, and I can't bear this anymore. I've got to get out of here, I need to run.

Mentally I measure the distance to the door. I just have to get that far, slam the heavy oak shut behind me, give myself a few extra seconds' head start—and hope that slamming the door doesn't prevent the chain from magically stretching again. Because if it pulls tight while I'm sprinting away, I'm going to break my neck.

On a soft prayer, I dart for the door.

A heavy body crashes into mine before I take three steps, knocking the air from my lungs, spinning me around—

And dumping me back onto the soft cushion of the bed.

I shriek in terror, ready to fight. Pinning my flailing hands, the giant figure looms over me, his dark hair a wild tangle, most of his face in shadow…

His face.

Abruptly my struggles stop, my heart squeezing tight in my chest. "Gideon?"

Eyes as green as spring meet mine, narrowing as they search my features. "When I dream of you, Cora Walker, you do not usually run from me."

I hardly recognize the voice that seems to reverberate

from deep within his chest before emerging on a rumbling growl.

I hardly recognize *him*—or the way he's gazing down at me. His eyes were always filled with warmth when he looked at me, but now they're glowing with heat, like glass drawn from a furnace.

More aware of the hard, muscular body leaning over mine than I've ever been aware of anything before, I ask breathlessly, "What do I usually do?"

His head dips toward mine, that thick tangle of hair smelling cold and crisp, like a night spent in the woods. I gasp as he buries his face against my neck, inhaling deeply. His mouth skims a burning line from the hollow of my throat to my jaw.

"Usually you're waiting for me in my bed, your soft thighs open and your body yearning for my touch." That roughened voice thickens. "The beast within me enjoyed it when you ran, Cora."

Oh god. The beast in *me* is enjoying the way he's holding me down, breathing in the scent of my skin. "Does he?"

Against my ear, Gideon makes a rumbling sound of assent. "But you smell far sweeter this time. As if you are not a dream at all."

Mind swimming in a haze of desire, I tell him, "I think I'm the one who is dreaming."

"Then I shall make you scream so loud that you will awaken." The gravelly promise in his voice is followed by the shock of his big hand pushing beneath my skirt. A

stunned breath catches in my throat, my body tensing—
then arching toward his on a ragged gasp when his long
fingers dip into my panties, delving through slippery
wetness and heat.

A tortured groan rips from his chest. "You are wetter
than I have ever dreamed. Shall I taste you, then, my
beautiful Cora? Shall I lick and tease your…your little…"

His body goes utterly still. His hand withdraws from
my panties, and when he pulls back, his fingers glisten
with the wetness of my arousal—and he's holding the glittering thread of the gold chain, which had been trapped
beneath my body when he tossed me onto the bed. I'm
still lying upon it, but now I feel the tug at the back of my
neck and the strange sensation of the line being pulled
up between my legs as Gideon raises it higher, his gaze
following the trailing length to the bedpost.

Abruptly he drops the chain and backs away, staring
at me with an expression near to horror. "You *are* here.
You've come." Torment darkens the green of his eyes and
he rips his hands through the long tangle of his hair, his
voice hardening, taut anger whitening his lips. "Bloody
fucking hell, Cora! You should *never* have come!"

I can't respond to that. Only sit up and scoot back to
the center of the bed, my body still aching with need and
my heart now trembling with fear.

Dried blood covers his hands. And his jaw and throat
and chest. He's naked, and almost every inch of his tall,
powerful form is filthy—his tanned skin not just covered

in blood but in dirt.

And his penis is erect.

Hugely erect.

I can hardly take my eyes off that long, thick cock. There's blood all over him, and I'm immobilized by uncertainty and terror, yet lust still has me in its merciless grip. My pussy clenches with desperate yearning as I stare at the blatant evidence of Gideon's desire for me.

A sardonic smile twists his firm lips. "And now there is the scent of your fear. It is also sweet to the beast." A cold, steely edge scrapes away the rough growl in his voice. "But not to me. Why did you come, Cora?"

"Mr. Singh. Your parents' solicitor." I struggle to pull coherent answers from the riot of emotions and thoughts crowding my mind. "He contacted me on their behalf."

"My parents were killed nine years ago." Over my gasp of disbelief and dismay, he asks, "Where is your father? He was supposed to protect you and keep you away from this place."

"He died this past fall." Raw grief aches in my throat. My father. His parents. "He had a stroke several years ago that left him bedridden. Then…he slowly faded."

A muscle working in his jaw, Gideon averts his face before saying gruffly, "I am sorry. He was a good man."

He was. But also a man who practically locked me away for years, away from everything and everyone I loved.

"I am sorry to hear about your parents, as well," I tell him softly. "They were always very kind to me."

"Kind to you?" A hard, short laugh barks from him. "Not at the end, if they gave Singh directions to bring you here. They must have left instructions to do it after your father passed."

"I don't know anything about that. Singh said there was a debt owed. I wasn't sure what it was—perhaps unpaid wages? But I came because I wanted to see Blackwood Manor again."

And to see Gideon again. But the man standing before me is not the same boy I knew. Not just because he's bigger, taller, stronger. Gideon had once been so kind and even tempered. Never had he shown the cold, cruel edge that Gideon has now, and never had he seemed so…feral.

Or so ravenous.

Nervously my gaze drops to his thick erection again—then rises to his broad chest, where blood has dried in smears and drips. *Drips*, as if he were a messy eater. And that deer had been torn apart. Yet how could a man do that?

I don't know *how* it's possible. But I also don't think I'm dreaming anymore.

"You came to see the estate?" A mocking smile appears on his lips. "And what do you think of Blackwood Manor today?"

My gaze snaps to his. "I think you should be ashamed of yourself."

Something pained flickers in the depths of those green eyes. "So I should be." Yet it is not contrition but arrogance that draws his angular features into hard, imposing lines.

"The debt owed was not *to* your father. It was a debt your father owed to me."

Gideon had only been seventeen when we'd left. What could my father owe a boy? "What are you talking about?"

"He took something of mine."

"You're saying my father *stole* something?" Firmly I shake my head. "He would never do that."

"I did not say he stole. I said he took what was mine." With a predator's fluid stride, he stalks silently to the edge of the bed, where he leans over and braces his hands on the mattress, his eyes on level with mine. Each word succinct, Gideon says, "He…took…my…bride."

His bride.

Hardly daring to breathe, I whisper, "Me?"

"Did you not agree to be mine?" Gaze holding mine, he winds the gold chain around his fist. "Did I not give you this necklace as I vowed to make you my wife? Did you not accept it?"

"I… I…" Of course I did. But bewilderment and fear prevent that admission. Because I don't understand any of this. "*Why* did he take me?"

"So that *this* would not happen. I told him to hide you away." He tugs gently on the chain, drawing me nearer, until my face is a breath from his. Softly he says, "But I have the key to release you, Cora."

"Then release me."

"Perhaps I will." Tormented gaze locked with mine, he skims the backs of his knuckles down the side of my face.

The growl deepens his voice as he adds, "But not yet."

Dropping the chain, he backs away again, abandoning me in the center of the bed, my heart wracked by hurt and confusion, my body alight with yearning and need.

Eyes hard, his gaze sweeps my length. "You are fortunate you did not arrive last night. You'd have received a much different reception."

How different? "Does that mean it would be better or worse?"

"Better for you or for me?" His eyes gleam with a hot and feral light. "Had I come upon you last night, I would have fucked you and made you mine—and I would have not cared whether you wanted me in return."

Not cared. I cringe away from those words. Away from this Gideon, who would not have cared for my feelings.

In response to my flinch, his cold laugh is a hateful sound. "So you cannot bear the thought of this touch?" He looks down at his bloodstained hands. "No matter. I have almost a month to persuade you to become mine in another way."

"What way?" I cry in frustration. "What are you talking about?"

He moves *so* fast. Abruptly his fingers are twisted in my hair, and he's kneeling in front of me on the bed, drawing my upper body against his chest, his mouth so close to mine.

"Cora Walker." My name from his lips is a low, thick rumble. "Will you get down on your hands and knees—and with love in your heart, offer the use of your cunt for my pleasure?"

My breath catches, and I stare at him in disbelief—and growing anger. "Why are you being so cruel?"

His cold green gaze searches mine. "I wonder if I am more cruel to you or to myself, to beg for your heart when I know you will deny me? And yet I cannot stop it. So I will ask this, as well, and we will see who is most hurt by it." Wrapping the gold chain around his bloodstained fingers, he gently tilts my chin higher, as if to ready my lips for his kiss. "Cora Walker...will you marry me?"

CHAPTER 2

Gideon

THE NEXT EVENING AS I sit adjacent to Cora at the dining table in the family wing, I ask her again.

"Will you marry me?"

Her answer is the same as it was when I asked her in my bed. Yet this time, her tears do not spill down her cheeks to land on my chest, each one like molten lead that blistered the surface of my heart.

Instead she calmly sips mushroom soup from her spoon before replying, "Release me from this chain, and we will see."

We will see. What I can see is Cora searching for escape. Even now, her beautiful blue eyes never meet mine, always looking elsewhere as if imagining herself away from me.

I *could* release her from the chain. Then she would run away from me, beyond the borders of this estate.

And I would die the moment she passed through the gate.

The curse that afflicts me and the magic that forms her chain make no logical, scientific sense—yet they are still governed by rules. My parents spared no expense, seeking answers…and a cure.

Answers they found. Rules were part of those answers. That there *is* no cure was another answer.

The beast is within me. Always, it will be within me.

Yet although there is no cure, there is control, for the heart and the soul of man and beast are one and the same. So if a man's heart is strong enough, if his will is great enough, he can control the beast…almost always. No matter how I fight, no matter how great my will, I cannot prevent the beast from emerging on the full moon.

But there is another way to tame the beast. For when it comes to love, the beast knows no reserve. A man might protect his heart; the beast does not. And a man's control over his heart is nothing compared to the power of a woman who owns it.

Just as Cora Walker owns mine. As she's owned it for the longest time.

The beast has always known of her, as if sensing her presence in the heart we share. He has always searched for her. Yet we'd kept her away, fearing the beast would find her.

Because that is another part of the curse—if a promise of love and marriage has been made, then the woman only has to draw near and she will be bound by that promise. I didn't know what form that binding would take, but it is the necklace I gave to her. Trapped by an innocent gift, given with the purest intentions.

Now my vow to marry Cora will destroy either her or me. Because the beast has scented her now. He's tasted her skin. She fills his heart as fully as she does mine.

Now he will fight to possess her. Yet if she gives herself to us in love, if she consents to be ours, then he will be content, and lie tame beneath her hand, only emerging if she is in danger or needs protection.

But if she leaves and shatters the heart we share, the beast will die.

And I will die with him.

If Cora ran from me, I would welcome death. Better than living with the scent of her always filling my lungs, better than living with the taste of her skin always upon my tongue, better than living without her. But I am not ready to die yet—and she will be safe here until the next full moon, when the beast within me will not give her any choice.

And if he takes her through force, forever will I remain the beast, because he will always struggle to possess her and will never relinquish control to me again. For now, I can keep him leashed. Yet if I should change forever, a beast driven by desperation to possess her…

Better for her that I will be dead.

I can feel that death approaching, bitter and cold. For years, living here alone, I thought I'd known bitterness, coldness. But they were nothing compared to having her here, knowing she will never be mine. Knowing the end is coming.

"So will you say yes to the other, then?" I ask of her. "Will you give yourself to me with love in your heart?"

Her baleful gaze meets mine. Flatly she says, "So that you may use my cunt for your pleasure?"

Her fragrant, juicy cunt. So wet and hot to the touch. Wetter and hotter than even in my fevered dreams. And the honeyed flavor of her juices that I licked from my bloodstained fingers was the sweetest heaven.

I would rip apart mountains simply to have one more taste. I would drag a star from the sky just for the chance to sip directly from the well of her cunt, to tease her clit with my tongue.

Cock aching with need, ravenous for another taste, I softly growl, "Yes."

Her response is silence, once again turning her beautiful face away from me.

I battle the urge to reach for her, to make her look at me. But I do not know how much control I have—and could not bear if she flinched away from my touch. So I use my voice to reach her, instead.

"Are you certain you wish to refuse?" When she still does not look at me but only takes another sip from her spoon, I tell her, "Your pussy wishes to be used for my pleasure. The moment I spoke of you giving yourself to me, the scent of your arousal bloomed like a flower. Even now, you are drowning in your own nectar."

Her wide, stunned gaze swings back to mine and she stares at me, pink embarrassment darkening her cheeks. "Why do you say such things?"

"Because they are true." Satisfied for the moment, now that her gaze is upon me, I lean back in my chair and reach for my wine. Its flavor is a poor, sour substitute for the sweet juices I'd rather taste upon my tongue. "I would ease that need for you. You do not have to get on your hands and knees tonight to take my cock. Instead sit upon this table and let me suck on your clit and feast from your cunt."

Between her full, parted lips, her breath comes in hot shallow pants. She stares at me, then looks away, then stares at me again. All the while her arousal fills the air with its rich, heady fragrance.

All the while the beast fights to emerge, wild to have her.

But the beast has not wanted Cora as long or as violently as I have, and his lust for her burns not nearly as hot as mine. The first time my fist ever wrapped around my cock, it was she who I pictured—at an age when I was still too young to truly understand what I wanted from her. By the time I was seventeen, I knew full well, and my desire for Cora was stronger than I ever let her know. Because she was still too young.

Now she is not. And all of these years, picturing how she would look—no longer a girl but a woman—my imaginings were but pale imitations of the beauty she had become. I had thought she would be all softness and curves, from the thick waves in her ash blond hair to the gentle swell of her belly to the sweep of her calves. Yet although the curves are there in the softness of her breasts and fullness of her lips, she's taut and lean, with an edge that sharpens her beauty to a painful degree.

With a shuddering breath, she tears her gaze from mine. Her fingers shake as she lifts another spoonful to her luscious mouth, then she asks quietly, "What happened to this place? Why is no one else here?"

"Because I sent the staff away." Those who had not already fled.

A little frown forms between her brows as she looks down at her soup. "Then who cooked this? And who brought the bread and cheese I ate for lunch?"

"Twice a week, Mrs. Collins leaves a basket for me outside the gate." Because I do not like to venture far outside the manor's grounds. The beast is territorial—and so I am now, too. Everything within the walls surrounding the estate is *mine*.

Everything outside those walls is none of my concern.

"Mrs. Collins?" Her gaze lifts to mine. "*Our* Mrs. Collins?"

The pleasure of hearing that word from her lips—*our*—is like a fierce, hot embrace around the hollow ache of my heart. "The same. She is still in my employ."

"But what of the others? Letting them go must have been a blow to the village economy."

So she will look at me while speaks of the manor and the people here. It is only when I speak of marrying her or of touching her that she turns her face.

Then I will always speak of the manor and its former staff. "I am not a savage," I tell her. "They all received severance packages large enough that they might retire, even if they were not of retiring age."

She laughs at that. "So? People don't want to do *nothing*. They want to be busy and useful. Well, most people do, anyway."

I narrow my eyes, trying to interpret her tone. "Do you refer to me?"

"I must. What do you do all day, Gideon? Because you are clearly not spending your time tending to your estate."

No, I do not. "I spend my days in the southeast tower. You are always welcome to come and see what I do there."

"I don't *care* what you do there," she abruptly snarls at me. "I only want you to release me."

Instantly the beast is right beneath my skin, urging me to take her, to make sure she can never leave. Struggling for control, I grit through clenched teeth, "Then agree to marry me."

She shoves her chair back. The chain trailing across the floor softly jingles against the marble tile and she freezes for the barest moment, despair tightening her lips—as if she had forgotten the chain was there until the sound reminded her.

Agony lurches through my chest. In one lunging stride, I am at her side, cupping her face in my hands, the beast roaring for me to ease her pain.

But we cannot let her go. Not yet.

Bending my head, I capture her mouth. She stiffens against me, then softens on a trembling sigh. Her lips part and I claim her with a possessive stroke of my tongue, the earthy flavor of the soup combining with her own luscious taste and overwhelming my senses with desperate hunger. Ravenously I feed from her lips, until she's clinging weakly to my arms and the scent of her arousal fills the air like the sweetest perfume.

Her blue eyes are soft and unfocused when I lift my mouth from hers, her lips red and swollen from our kiss, her nipples standing stiff beneath the thin fabric of her blouse. And although everything within me—man and beast—clamors to take her now, that is not what we need from her.

"Tomorrow," I growl against her lips, "your answer will be yes."

HER ANSWER IS THE SAME, tossed carelessly at me over a meal of roast guinea hen. "Release me first."

Not yet. But I say nothing, cold bitterness digging into my throat with arid, icy claws—hot irritation prickling my skin. The beast does not like clothes, but I have taken to wearing them again now that Cora is here. Though I do not wear much. The beast would not tolerate shoes or underpants. But even a soft cotton shirt and my ancient jeans seem to chafe and constrict every movement.

As if heading me off before I can ask her to get down on her hands and knees, she asks, "My luggage is out by the east access gate. Can you get it for me tomorrow?"

"I already collected your suitcase." Drawn there by her scent as I'd run a course through the grounds, because the open air pleases both me and the beast. "I took it to your bedchamber this afternoon."

A chamber in the northwest wing—as far from mine as she could get.

"Thank you," she says absently, poking at her meal. "What else did you do today?"

"I watched you."

Her head jerks up and her widened gaze meets mine. "From where?"

From a distance, because I wasn't certain of my control. The beast has become more insistent since she arrived. "The northeast tower."

"You said you stayed all day in the southeast tower."

"That was before you risked choking yourself to death."

Because today she tested the length of the chain, walking across the great lawn. A few paces away from the main gates, the chain had gone taut, stopping her short. Yet still she'd pulled against it, futilely trying to break the links or make them stretch farther, until she crumpled to the ground in a sobbing heap.

The beast's claws dug gouges into the stone sill as we'd watched, knowing we could cross the distance quickly if she hurt herself, terrified she would. And it was I who held us back, because I didn't know whether I would be the one in control as we rushed to her side. If the beast emerged…he would not stop at easing the chain's pull upon her neck. He would not stop until he made her his.

Listlessly she pushes a carrot around her plate with a fork. "The chain won't let me leave the grounds."

"No. It won't." Not until I rescind my vow to marry her.

She raises accusing eyes to mine. "*You* won't let me leave. You *could* free me."

"Yes," I agree softly. "But I won't."

Her jaw clenches and her lips tremble as she stares at me with hatred shining from the blue of her eyes. Abruptly she pushes away from the table, collecting her dishes to carry into the kitchen.

"I *will* let you leave the room," I tell her. "Does that please you?"

She hurls her plate at my head.

I HAVE ALWAYS LOVED THAT Cora is a fighter. I've always loved that she never gives up.

But I cannot bear another day of watching this.

The beast urges me to run as I cross the great lawn, and I give in to that urge, my focus tight on Cora's figure ahead, never allowing him to break through my skin.

Each of her sobbing, gasping breaths rips a gaping

hole into my heart. The long golden chain is tense as a wire, stretching from her nape to the hall in the distance, yet she's still straining against it. Fighting.

Let her fight me, instead.

Roughly I snag my arm around her waist and swing her up against my chest. "That's enough!"

"Let me go!" She screams as I begin carrying her back toward the manor house. Instantly the tension on the chain eases. "Damn you, Gideon. Go back!"

Her voice is hoarse, from choking or sobbing or both. Bruises ring her neck, and her skin is raw and reddened. There's not a chance in hell that I'll let her go and I'm not turning back.

Her fists land solid blows against my shoulders. Wild kicks send sharp pains shooting through my shins.

The beast *loves* it. My cock is a thick iron bar that grows hotter and harder with every blow she lands.

I don't love it. Not when her ragged sobs accompany every hit, not when her struggles rapidly weaken until she's lying limp against my chest, weeping helplessly against my shoulder.

"You will *never* do this again." Forced through the raw ache of my throat, the command is harsh and thick. "If you do, I will lock the doors so that you cannot even leave the house."

"Then I will jump from a window!"

Cold fear pierces my skin, the beast trying to claw through the holes her words ripped in me. "Do not even say such a thing!" I roar and when she flinches against me, burying her face against my throat, I have to fight for the calm before I speak again. "Would you?"

In a quiet voice, she says, "No."

Yet it must have crossed her mind. Hoarsely I ask, "Do you want to escape me so badly?"

"I want to be *free!*" Despair fills her cry and she pounds her fist against my chest. "Do you not understand the difference?"

I do. But I can't let her go yet.

And at least she is fighting again. "Will you marry me, Cora?"

"Fuck off," she says.

FOR DAYS, CORA TAKES HER meals to her chambers instead of joining me at the table. As the moon wanes and March becomes April, my time with her grows shorter—but she is not completely absent. I watch her from the tower as she spends each day working in the south garden, and although she rarely strays from the northwest wing, the entire house is filled with her scent. Each breath I take carries her into me, her sweet fragrance—tinged with the cold bitterness I know too well after years spent alone.

With every step, that loneliness hangs around her like a shroud.

Perhaps that is why she finally joins me again. This time I do not immediately ask her to marry me, but allow the tension to ease out of the silence between us—and allow her the first word.

It comes near the end of the meal, when she quietly asks, "What happened to your dad and mum?"

"They were killed."

She looks up, her eyes meeting mine. The soft reluctance in those blue depths grips my heart, touched by her regret that she has asked and caused me pain. Yet determination shines there, too. "How?"

I lean back in my chair and unflinchingly return her stare. "Do you think I did it?"

Her gaze shifts away from mine—not in an admission of guilt, but so she can pensively study the walls, the faint bloodstains left on the rug, the shattered mirror, and the divan with its upholstery slashed in parallel stripes. "No," she finally says. "I don't know what to think of many things, beginning with the slaughtered deer in the grove, or the blood that was all over your face and hands. But never once has it occurred to me that you were the one who killed your parents. Though now I wonder if I should question it? Yet I still don't. I don't think you could have ever hurt them."

The shield I had slapped over my heart, preparing for the stabbing wounds of her accusation and doubt, crumbles into nothing as those knives never appear. Yet my chest still feels pierced through. She has no reason to still have faith in me, to believe in me. Yet she does, and it's everything I can do not to reach for her, to draw her close.

"I did not," I tell her through a throat that feels hot

and swollen. "They were attacked by the same monstrous bastard who chased us on your birthday."

A murderous fiend who'd claimed Blackwood Manor as part of his territory while my parents and I searched for answers regarding the curse. When we returned, he came to kill me. He ran across my parents first.

Her lips part. "There was really someone out there that night? I told myself afterward that it only *seemed* so terrifying. And that it'd really been a wild boar or some feral dog."

That is what I needed her to believe—and could hardly believe the truth myself. But I had seen the howling nightmare that lunged at me as I'd forced my way through the gap in the gate. I'd seen the gleaming fangs, and the claws that ripped into my leg. It had been past midnight, but the moon had been full and high and bright, and I'd recognized what had come after us.

A myth. A legend. Something out of a horror film, not something real.

Yet it had been.

And I'd known what it was, but I could not bear her terror. So I'd laughed with her, teased her as we'd made our way back to the manor house, all the while feeling the beast's curse winding its way through my blood.

My parents believed my claim that a werewolf had attacked us, but I didn't have to convince them—or Cora's father. The security cameras mounted atop the estate wall had captured everything.

"So he came back?" she whispers now.

"He came back."

"And killed them?" Her eyes swim with tears.

"Yes."

"Were you here?"

Slowly I nod. Though it had been during the full moon, so it was not only me. My beast had been out hunting on the estate grounds and heard their screams.

"What happened?"

"This time I was stronger than he was," I say simply.

Her trembling lips press together as she looks tearfully around the room again. "Is that when all of this damage happened? And in the parlor…and the other rooms… and your bedchamber…"

She trails off, as if recognizing even as she spoke how little sense that made.

"They were outside," I tell her. "This…was something else."

The beast, returning from his hunts bloodied and sated with raw meat, yet still searching for what he knew was missing. Because he had memories of her, too, *my* memories of her in every room. And he had torn each chamber apart in his frustration when he could never find her.

But what the beast had done in this wing was nothing compared to the damage he'd done to the gatehouse. He'd torn apart the very floorboards in his search for the missing half of his soul.

I still awaken in her garden after every full moon,

naked and half-buried in the dirt, as if he'd tried to cover himself in the same soil he knew she'd once touched—or as if praying she might come and tend to him as she had once tended to everything that was ever planted there.

And each time, he dug holes that destroyed more and more of what she'd left behind. Hating himself for it, as *I* hated him for it.

Yet still unable to help himself.

But I will not awaken in her garden on the morning after the next full moon. If she cannot accept us, I will not awaken at all. And the beast will never destroy anything of hers again.

Those icy, bitter fingers wrap around my heart. I try to warm it with a swallow of burgundy, but wine is still not what I want on my tongue. "You've made progress in your garden."

"You watched that from your tower, too?" The same cold bitterness clutching at my heart fills her reply. "You should have come down and helped me."

Though she had avoided me for days? "Do you truly want me so near to you?"

"Why wouldn't I?" she challenges. "Will you hurt me?"

"It is not hurt you have to fear." Not with me. Though the beast wants exactly what I want, and dreams of what I do.

Of Cora on her knees. Of mounting her, burying our thick cock in the burning depths of her cunt, and listening to her cries echo through every chamber in the house as we fuck her relentlessly. With me, those cries would be of need and pleasure.

With him, she would likely be screaming in pain and fear.

Her mouth set in a stubborn line, she reaches for her wine. "Then why should I worry if you are near to me?"

"Because every time I come near to you, your body readies to take me," I tell her harshly. "Because the sweet petals of your pussy open and perfume the very air with your nectar. Because the tight buds of your nipples seek my touch as a flower seeks the touch of the sun. And you have said again and again that you have no wish to give yourself to me with love in your heart, or to allow me the use of your cunt for my pleasure. But if I was so near to you throughout the day, Cora, how long would it be before you were on your hands and knees in the dirt of that garden, *begging* me to plow my cock deep?"

Cheeks flushed, she draws a trembling breath. "I would not."

No, she would probably not. Not my stubborn Cora. No matter how much she wants, not matter how wet she is, not matter how deep the ache.

It would be I—and the beast—who would end up begging…or taking. Even now he tries to tear his way through, my fingernails lengthening, my eyeteeth sharpening. But the painful hardness of my cock is all mine, my hunger and need for her endless.

Yet still he fights to the surface, and my voice is a low, growling rumble as I command, "Marry me."

Her steady blue gaze locks with mine and she makes a demand of her own. "Free me."

Not yet, I would have said, but instead the beast roars, "*NEVER!*"

Cora rears back in her chair, eyes flying wide. Afraid.

I grip the edge of the heavy oak table, claws gouging the surface, fighting for control. *She's afraid.* That is all the beast sees, and he rips at my skin, trying to emerge and protect her.

He doesn't understand she needs protecting from *this.*

With all of my will, I battle the overwhelming urge to let him take over, to let him shield her, my hands tightening on the table's edge as I silently wage war against the beast within.

Then the silence is broken with a great, splintering crack. Cora gasps as the table splits down the center. Her hands fly to her mouth to muffle a disbelieving cry.

Disbelief and surprise. Not fear.

The beast begins to recede.

Cora stares at me over her fingers. "Well," she whispers shakily, "now I know what happened to all of the furniture."

Perhaps for the best. Because if there was anything of this table left, I would bend her over it and drive the full length of my cock into her sweet silky heat, making her scream in pleasure as I ease this agonizing need—as I fill her womb with my hot seed.

The beast and I are not always so different.

And this time I am the first to get up and leave.

WITH THE BEAST'S ACUTE SENSES attuned to Cora's every move, I'm always aware of where she is and what she's doing, even if she's in another wing of the house or at the edge of the estate.

This morning it rained, so instead of working in the garden, she retreated to the library and spent several quiet hours. I was aware of her soft tread leaving that chamber and heading toward the southeast wing, but I expected that she would veer toward the family kitchen. Instead she paused at the bottom of the tower stairs and began to climb, her steps steadily rising and the slithering jingle of the chain following.

Cora almost reaches the tower chamber before I accept that she truly *is* coming to see me. Not hesitating, not retreating. Hurriedly I drag on my jeans, and the beast is so excited by her approach that he does not even protest the confining cloth.

The heavy wooden door to the tower chamber is always open, so I see her the moment she ascends to the top of the spiraling staircase. She's dressed in her own beauty, her pale blond hair in a loose braid over her shoulder, her full lips pink, her narrow feet bare. The skirt she wore the day she arrived conceals the long, taut muscles of her thighs, the hem kissing her knees with every step. A sleeveless shirt hugs her ribs and full breasts.

I do not bother with my own shirt. I barely bother with the zip of my jeans. Instead I quickly comb my fingers through my hair, and greet her with a smile that cannot hope to tell her how much pleasure this unexpected visit has given me.

The sky blue of her gaze does not lift to my face, however. With warm color staining her cheeks, she glances at my abdomen before quickly turning away, indicating the stairs with a sweep of her hand. "I'd forgotten how many steps there were! Do you remember when we used to race up to this chamber?"

I remember everything about her. "Yes."

Her gaze is unfocused and her smile is sweet, lost to those memories—then abruptly it sharpens.

"Did you let me win?"

"Sometimes." And sometimes jostling against her in the narrow confines of the stairwell aroused my teenaged body so much that running had seemed an agony.

My teenaged body knew *nothing* of agony. For nothing I felt then could compare to now.

"Until the day I tripped and twisted my ankle."

"And I carried you down to the solarium." Feeling like a hero…and hating myself for letting her be hurt in the first place.

"Then refused to race me again," she says with her eyes narrowing on me—then she abruptly stops at the entrance to the chamber, wonder filling her expression.

For an endless time she does nothing but look, her bare feet carrying her farther into the chamber, slowly turning so that she can see the canvases hanging from every wall.

"Gideon," she breathes in awe. "Did you paint these?"

"I did."

In disbelief she shakes her head. "You were never this good before."

"I've had more opportunity to practice."

She pauses in front of a landscape—the gatehouse, as it had looked when she and her father lived there. Before the gates were closed and chained. "So this is where you spend most of your time?"

"Yes." This chamber soothes me…and soothes the beast. For he is often content to be surrounded by reminders of the love I'd known instead of searching for what is no longer here.

Not content today, though. Not with Cora here. Instead our need for her rages hotter than ever, the scent of her filling this chamber, the sound of her soft breaths in our ears, the taste of her skin only a step and a lick away.

She smiles over a portrait of herself, looking fierce and determined, a cricket bat at ready in her grip. And another of her bulging cheeks full of Mrs. Collins's stolen scones, wide-eyed and tight-lipped from the effort of trying not to laugh, and with crumbs clinging to her shirt.

"Was that the day we received The Great Lecture?" she says it in the same manner the lecture had been delivered, as if state secrets were hidden in the scones we'd stolen.

"It was."

"Oh," she exclaims quietly, standing in front of another painting. "Your dad and mum."

As I remember them best—walking hand-in-hand

through Cora's garden, with the sun upon their faces.

She glances back at me, at my face and lower, then quickly away—and abruptly stills with her gaze arrested by the large painting on the east wall. As if in a trance, she moves closer, whispering, "What is this?"

"A dream," I tell her.

Unlike all of the others, not something from my past. Simply Cora, lying upon a bed in a room filled with sunshine, her body soft and supple…and waiting for me.

"This is in your bedchamber—as it used to be?"

"Yes."

Puzzlement creases her brow and she glances back. "Why was your bed not destroyed? Everything else was."

Because the bed was the only thing in my bedchamber that she'd never been in. Everything else, she'd touched— the desk, the chairs, even the wardrobe, on those days when our adventures would leave her in desperate need of a clean shirt to borrow.

She does not wait for my answer but studies the painting again. "Have you watched me sleep?"

I have. But—"This was painted before you came back."

A bitter smile curves her lips. "So that is why you do not show me chained to the bed."

A growl rises from my chest. "And because the woman in that painting has already given herself to me with love in her heart. So I would have already released her."

"Then how can you be certain it was love and not desperation that drove her to accept you?"

"Because she *stayed*," I tell her. "Would you?"

"You'll have to release me first to find out. Will you?"

"No."

Eyes glittering, she turns away from me—away from the painting. She pauses over a portrait of herself standing in the moonlight, her lips freshly kissed. A new diamond pendant shines from the hollow of her throat. Her blue eyes glittered with tears then, too. But they were joyous, hopeful.

Cora's breath shudders and she moves quickly on. The silence between us deepens as she continues studying each painting, yet her attention on them seems more and more unfocused as she goes—her gaze straying to me often, the flush never leaving her cheeks.

Because I've been aroused since hearing her first step at the bottom of the tower stairs, and I hardly bothered to zip.

"If you want to look at my cock, then only say so," I tell her. "And I will give you a better view than this."

Her blush deepening, she freezes in place—her eyes closing.

That won't do.

I stalk closer. Her eyes fly open again at the short rasp that sounds as I unzip the few inches I'd fastened in haste. She takes a quick step back. Not far. Her shoulders press up against a painting of her garden, a canvas bursting with light and color.

She goes utterly still as I take the aching length of my

cock in my right hand, her gaze fixed on my fist. Bracing my left palm against the wall beside her shoulder, I watch her face and slowly stroke my straining shaft, a rumbling groan reverberating in my chest.

"Gideon," she breathes. I cannot tell if it is supposed to be a protest or shock or encouragement, but the sound of my name upon her tongue is like fire over my skin.

In a voice roughened by need, I tell her, "Did you think I would react in any other way when you are so close? Just as your cunt blossoms for me when I am near." And she has been near me so long, the scent of her arousal is in full bloom. "Now watch me come for you."

Breasts lifting as she drags in a ragged breath, she watches me, her tongue darting out to moisten her parted lips, her own hands fisted.

"Do you imagine what I imagine?" Gritting my teeth, I stroke harder. "That this is not my hand, but instead your wet pussy rides my length. That my cock fills your hot cunt and we are racing together, trying to come."

Softly she moans, her back arching against the canvas, her hips canting toward me. Her fingers flex.

"Come with me, Cora. Rub your sweet clit, as I know you do in your bed."

Her gaze flies up to mine, but instead of the outrage I expect, there's only hot temptation in the blue flame of her eyes.

Arm rigidly braced beside her shoulder, I bend my head closer to hers, my chest heaving with deep breaths that match the long stroke of my hand. "The first time I ever did this, I thought of you. The last time I did this, I thought of you. I have *only* thought of you, Cora. Never another woman."

Her breath catches. "Never?"

It shouldn't even be a question. "I vowed to marry you. What kind of man would ever look at another?"

Even the beast within me would not.

Her gaze falls to my cock again. "No one else has ever touched you?"

"Never."

She bites her lip. "May I?"

Ah fuck. At that shyly spoken request, my cock pulses hard in my grip. Quickly letting go, I grit my teeth and fight the need to come before she even touches me. "You need not ask permission," I growl softly. "I am yours to use for your pleasure."

Hesitantly she reaches for me. A tortured groan rips from my throat at the first soft touch—her fingertips gliding up the underside of my straining shaft.

My head bows, exquisite agony drawing every muscle tight as she takes a firmer grip, stepping closer to wrap both hands around the base of my throbbing length.

"Like this?" she asks breathlessly, stroking from root to tip.

My response is a hiss of breath through clenched teeth. "Yes."

"Good." Her soft pants punctuate the rise and fall of

her hands. The fragrance of her arousal deepens, thickens, until I can almost taste her pussy juices with every breath. "Because I haven't done this before, either."

Head jerking up, I stare at her flushed face. She's watching her hands working the ruddy length of my erection as if mesmerized by the sight. "You haven't what? Wanked a man's cock?"

I can't stop the deepening rumble of my voice at the thought of her with someone else. But that was the price of protecting her, sending her away—knowing I would not be her first. Knowing I would not be her only.

And I survived these years by *never* imagining her with another man.

"Touched anyone else," she whispers. "Only you."

Only me. The knowledge burns through my brain like a lightning strike, the beast rising so hard, so fast, his triumphant roar filling my chest and my cock spasming in her grip. The orgasm blazes through me, my teeth gritted as every muscle in my body stiffens, her gasp of surprise joining the hot splash of cum against my rigid abdomen.

"Oh," Cora whispers, staring. "Oh my—"

She breaks off with a strangled cry as I drop to my knees and shove her skirt high. My claws shred her panties, her luscious scent filling my nostrils. Maddened by lust for this cunt, this cunt that will *only* be mine, I take my first taste, spreading her labia with my thumbs and licking those glistening pink lips with a roughened tongue.

Body going rigid, Cora makes a thick, guttural noise

low in her throat as her sultry flavor explodes through my senses. Her fingers fist in my hair.

Groaning as her delicious juices fill my mouth, I lick deeper, parting those sweet petals, seeking the source of her nectar, thrusting my stiffened tongue past her virgin entrance.

Legs trembling, she whimpers softly, rocking her pussy against my mouth. "My clit. Oh god, my clit."

I would tease her longer. I would savor this first taste. But the beast is desperate for her release, to give her anything she needs, everything she asks for.

Ravenously I latch onto her slick bud, sucking and licking, her wild moans of pleasure echoing in my ears. With one broad finger I tease at her entrance, until she cries out "Please!" and I breach that untouched channel, her inner muscles clutching tightly as I push deep.

Raggedly moaning my name, she stiffens and rises onto her toes. I follow her up, feasting upon her clit, gently fucking her virgin cunt with long, slow thrusts of my finger.

She comes silently but her body is a riot of pleasure, her muscles shaking and her pussy convulsively grasping my finger, her clit throbbing against my tongue and her nectar flooding my mouth. Growling against her sweet flesh, I devour the juices from the well of her cunt before hungrily returning to her clit.

And demanding more.

Her breath shudders in sobbing gasps when she comes again. Her body sags back against the wall, and she weakly pushes at my head after I lap her up and return to her clit. "No more. I can't."

I could, forever. But now there's more that I want.

Gripping her tight bottom, I rise to my feet and lift her against me. Automatically her long legs wrap around my waist, and I deliberately rub the seed from my stomach against the wet heat of her cunt, until our scents are melded into one.

Marking her as mine. Marking me as hers.

Twisting my fingers in her hair, I bring her passion-spent gaze to mine. "Marry me, Cora."

On a soft sigh, she wreathes her arms around my neck, burying her fingers in my hair—as if to make certain I cannot look away. Her blue eyes slowly clear as she searches my face. "Do you mean, marry you and stay here forever in an empty house, with a husband who hides away all day?"

Her words are like fangs tearing open my throat. "I do not *hide*. With these paintings, I can hold on to everything that has gone. I can keep alive every*one* that has gone."

"And in the meantime, everything they left behind— and everything they built—falls to ruins, destroyed by your neglect." She releases her grip on my hair and gently traces the line of my jaw. "Is this what you offer me, then? A husband who remains mired in the past instead of looking toward the future?"

I have not much of a future to look toward. But perhaps it is not *my* future that matters. With a burning lump lodged in my throat, I ask, "So if this estate were as it was before, would you marry me then?"

"Release me and perhaps you will find out."

Never. The beast's response remains trapped in my aching chest, but it is no different from mine. Because I never want to let her go.

But I have to.

Softly she asks, "Will you give me the key, Gideon?"

"No," I tell her hoarsely, though it is a lie.

Because the only other choice is to see her hurt. Better that she runs from me. Better that I die.

If the price of her freedom is to give my own life, I *will* pay it.

But not yet.

"Well, then." With tears pooling in her blue eyes, she lets her legs drop from around my waist and gently pushes away from me. "We have nothing else to say. And you have given me no reason to *ever* marry you."

Except that I love her. And that I have always loved her.

I don't think she would believe it, though. Not when I keep her here, chained to me. That is not love, she would say.

And the cost of proving my love is to die. But perhaps there is another way to show her.

In despair I watch her leave the tower, then listen to her retreating steps, to the slithering of that cursed chain. The beast rages at me to follow, but he is at his weakest now. The new moon rises tonight.

She has been at Blackwood Manor for two weeks. Two weeks remain until the moon is full.

So I have two weeks to give her reason to marry me. Two weeks to hope that everything I do will make her love me in return.

Or two weeks until I let her go…and watch her run away, taking my heart—and my life—with her.

CHAPTER 3

Cora

I WAKE UP THE MORNING of my twenty-fifth birthday with the sun streaming through my bedchamber's sparkling windows and warming the gleaming floor. No more dust. No more cobwebs. Two weeks ago, Gideon threw open the manor's gates—then hired nearly every handyman and housecleaning service within fifty miles to come and polish the interior of the house into a shining jewel. Gardeners and landscapers have transformed the grounds. Those have not been restored to their former glory—only time will do that—but the air of neglect is gone. Flowers provide bursts of color and perfume and new sod has been lain, the spring grass as green as Gideon's eyes.

Only the south garden was left untouched because, as

Gideon told me, that garden is mine.

All of this, he'd done to persuade me to marry him.

Every night, he asks me. Every night, I long to say yes.

But the chain still circles my neck, and if I accept his proposal just to buy my release, then I will be saying yes for the wrong reasons. A woman should be free to choose to marry. Not choosing to marry because that's the only way to be free.

So I give Gideon the same answer—that I will tell him after he releases me. And each time I give that answer, the brilliant light in his eyes seems to fade. As if with every night that passes, he loses hope that I'll ever accept him.

But he has also not touched me since the day in his tower, so perhaps it is not only his hope that fades. Perhaps his desire for me is waning, too.

A thought that claws at my heart, digging into my chest until it hurts to breathe. Miserably I curl up beneath the blankets, picturing the version of Cora in his painting who is already free and awaiting Gideon in his bedchamber, eager to love him with her body and soul.

The Cora who stayed.

I would stay. But *staying* means nothing if I don't have the choice to go, and although the gates are open, the chain still would not allow me to pass through them. So he has to release me first.

But I'm beginning to think he never will.

A gentle tug at the back of my neck brings me out of my miserable cocoon. I poke my head out from beneath the blankets.

Wearing jeans and a black T-shirt, Gideon stands at the entrance to my bedchamber, his brooding gaze fixed on the chain wrapped around his fist. "You were not at breakfast, so I followed this to find you." His eyes lift to meet mine, and concern warms his gaze as he studies my face. "Are you well, Cora?"

He doesn't need to follow that chain to find me. Somehow he *always* knows where I am. It's another part of the mystery of this new Gideon, who is at once the boy I loved and a stranger I've fallen for all over again. This new Gideon who can rip apart solid oak, and who somehow possesses the key to a magical golden collar with no lock.

"I'm well," I tell him and it's not a complete lie. My body is fine.

It's my heart that's sick.

"Yet you still lie abed." Silently he prowls closer, and sudden tension prickles my skin. Because there's something different about him this morning. Something taut and wild, sharper than the feral edge he's gained as this new Gideon. Something more like he was that first day, when he was covered in dirt and blood.

That is not the only the only difference in him, though I can't immediately pin the other down. But whatever I'm sensing in him, it knots in my belly, heavy with despair and dread.

I sit up. "Are *you* all right?"

He doesn't answer as he reaches the side of the bed.

Instead he cups my cheek in a gentle hand, his thumb sweeping over my lips. "Do you linger in bed in hopes of a breakfast tray appearing? After all, it is your birthday."

Joy fills my heart, unknotting the dread. "You remembered?"

"I could hardly forget." Something dark passes through his expression before he focuses on me again, his gaze searching mine. "So shall I pamper you today, Cora?"

I grin. "Yes, please."

"Then you will be pampered. And on this day, I will not ask anything of you." Abruptly his mouth lowers to mine, and he says gruffly against my lips, "I will only give."

Starting with the sweetest kiss. Then giving pleasure, as the kiss deepens and heats, until I'm whimpering and clinging to him in desperate need. And giving more, slowly making his way down, worshipping my breasts and teasing my nipples into fiery points of arousal. Tasting the taut skin of my belly, until I'm quivering with anticipation, and finally moving lower, pushing my legs wide to make room for his shoulders as he settles between my trembling thighs.

Then he gives me another kiss, one that doesn't end, even as I writhe and scream and convulse against his tongue. After I collapse back against the pillows, shaking, he gives a few seconds' respite—then claims me with his mouth again, fingers thrusting deep as he lashes my clit with merciless teasing licks.

The second orgasm he gives builds slowly before

crashing over me in a devastating wave that leaves me boneless and sated—unable to do anything but simply lie in my bed with him, threading my fingers through his thick hair when he pillows his head against the softness of my stomach, holding me tight.

Thinking I know the reason he's holding me so tightly, I try to urge him up over me again. "Let me taste *you* this time, Gideon."

On a rough groan, his body goes utterly rigid—then he abruptly pulls away. Pushing his hands through his hair, he stares at me with blatant hunger, his cock a thick bulge behind denim.

"Not today," he says hoarsely and the bleak despair that flattens his gaze twists that knot tight inside my chest again. "Today is only for you."

I reach for him. "That *would* be for me—"

"Not today." He closes his eyes as if to shut out the sight of me, naked and yearning for him. "I barely have any bloody control as it is."

"Good. The point would be to make you lose it completely." Just as his mouth completely destroys *my* control.

He barks out a short laugh. "You don't know what you ask for." Then, shaking his head, he turns away. "Stay right there in bed, birthday girl. I'll bring your breakfast tray."

"I'd rather you feed me something else!" I call after him.

His long strides never falter. He vanishes into the corridor, and I'm left staring after him, feeling utterly lost.

Then utterly bewildered, when I glance down—and

spot the parallel slashes tearing through the white linen bed sheet on either side of my hips.

THE CHAIN FEELS HEAVIER TODAY. Oftentimes I barely even notice it. The links never catch on any objects and pull me up short. If I have to thread it down the back of my shirt, such as when I'm wearing a T-shirt that I pull over my head instead of a button-up blouse, the chain seems content to lie against my skin. Even when the house was busy with people cleaning, it never seemed to get in anyone's way despite trailing across the floor from one wing to the other.

Not today. Today it seems to deliberately lie in my path to trip me. Today it catches on practically every leg of furniture I pass. Today it gets trapped in the shower drain, and as I dress it tangles in my hair, yanking painfully at my scalp. As if trying to slow me down, to halt my every step. As if to keep me from going anywhere.

As if it hadn't already been doing that for almost a month.

So after Gideon brings my breakfast, I'm slow to get started. Then we have lunch together in the solarium, where my dessert is another long, languid orgasm, with Gideon feasting from my lips as his thumb strums my clit and his fingers sink deep into my virgin sheath. And just as before, when I try to touch him, he abruptly leaves me alone, hungrily licking my pussy juices from his fingers as he goes.

It's long into the afternoon when I finally make my way down to the garden—where the chain promptly snags on a rosebush, and I spend a frustrating fifteen minutes trying to get free.

And I know it's not natural behavior. Not that the chain is natural in *any* sense—just as so much here at Blackwood Manor is no longer natural in any sense—but before today, the chain only passively prevented me from passing beyond the estate's property line. Now it seems to be actively preventing me from going anywhere. And it can't be a coincidence that the chain begins behaving in this way on my birthday, the anniversary of the day he originally gave me the necklace as a gift.

On the same day Gideon claims to have no control and leaves claw marks in my bed. The same day the knot of dread in my gut won't untwist. It all adds up to *something*, but I don't know what that something is.

But there is something I *do* know. Because as irritating as the golden binding is, as much as I hate it…if wearing this chain was the price I had to pay to stay with Gideon forever, I would pay it.

Yet he *can* release me. So I don't understand why he doesn't. I would stay either way.

Though perhaps the tower where he spent so much time partially answers that question. Because the only thing clear about this whole insane situation is that Gideon has lost far too much, and he's spent years desperately trying to hold on to memories of a happier time.

Now he's holding on to me instead of setting me free—
as if he's afraid of losing me again.

Does he truly not know that I wouldn't go? That this
is my home, has always been my home, and my place has
always been at his side?

I just want to be free. Not free of *him*.

And that is what I'll tell him when he finds me again.
Because he promised pampering today, but there's nothing
more luxurious than spending time with my hands in
the soil—and only the pleasure Gideon gives to me sur-
passes the joy of bringing this garden back to perfumed,
colorful life. When I'd first arrived here at the manor, I'd
seen this garden and believed there was no place for me
here anymore. But with every new bud and bloom, I'm
more certain than ever that this will always be my home.
It was just waiting for me to return.

The sun is low in the sky when movement near the
house catches my eye. Gideon, approaching the garden
with his face drawn into harsh lines and his eyes burning a
fiery green, as if witnessing the torments in the pits of Hell.

His demand is a rumbling crack of thunder. "Where
have you been?"

In confusion, I look around me. "Where else would
I be?"

"I have searched for you for two *hours*." Gideon crosses
the garden to stand before me. "I couldn't hear where you
were, couldn't find your scent. And *this* bloody thing"—he
grips the chain dangling from my neck—"led me through

every fucking room in the house!"

I tell him, "It's being weird today." And so is he. "Of course I'm out here. When am I not?"

"Today. You shouldn't be *here* at all." His voice is hoarse as he cups my face in his hands, his gaze wildly searching mine. "I have more to give you. And I hadn't wanted to rush but we're out of time."

"Okay," I say slowly, trying to calm the panic that's rising within me, witnessing his urgency. "Do you have the gifts with you or do we need to go inside?"

"It's inside. It's outside." Turning, he sweeps his arm in a half circle, as if indicating the garden—or beyond. "It's all of this. Blackwood Manor."

"What? How can it be mine?"

"I had the paperwork drawn up this week. It will all be yours."

Is this another proposal? "What do you mean, exactly?"

"I don't have any family to leave it to. And in my heart, you have always been my wife." His tormented gaze burns into mine. "So if something happens to me...it's yours."

"*Nothing* is going to happen to you." Even the joy of hearing him call me his wife can't overcome the pain of what he followed it with. My chest aches at the very thought of him being hurt...or worse. "And I don't want that gift. Not if I get it like that."

"You'll take it," he growls the command fiercely, "because I wouldn't trust the property to anyone else. And I have something more to give you."

I'm not sure I want any more of his gifts. "What do you—"

But I'll take *this*. His mouth claims mine, his hands capturing my face and drawing me close against his hard chest. Tender and sweet, filled with a longing that brings tears to my eyes, his kiss feels like a declaration of love and home and forever.

My throat's clogged with emotion as he draws away, winding the golden chain around his fist.

"Cora Walker," he says in a voice so hollow that each word seems to echo from an empty space in his chest, "the promise I made when I gave you this necklace…that vow means nothing. I have no intention of marrying you now."

Breathless with pain, I stare mutely at him.

"My final gift is your freedom," he continues harshly. "Now get the hell away from Blackwood Manor."

Freedom…?

I lift shaking fingers to my neck. The chain is gone. Instead it dangles from his fist…but it's just a necklace and a diamond pendant again. Just a piece of jewelry.

A piece of jewelry that means *nothing*. Feeling as if my entire world is tearing apart, I raise blurry eyes to his. "Gideon?"

"*Go*, Cora." Face tormented, he backs away from me. "Damn my selfish heart. I said that today I would only give, but in truth I was taking every moment for myself. One last day. But I should have sent you away the same hour you arrived."

"But why?" My voice cracks. *"Why?"*

"Just get out of here."

Tears spilling down my cheeks, wildly I shake my head.

"Get out!" he roars.

A sob breaks from me. "But I have nowhere to go. This is my only home."

Pain slashes across his face. "Then run to the village," he tells me hoarsely. "I don't care, as long as you're anywhere but here. Because I *never* want you to step foot on this estate again—not as long as I live."

Each word shatters my heart. With my hands flying to my mouth to muffle my agonized cry, I flee from him, blinded by tears. But this is my home, and every step so familiar that I make my way to my bedchamber in the northwest wing without any memory of getting there. With sobs ripping from my chest, I begin throwing clothes into my suitcase, but don't even get it half full before I crumple to the floor, bawling helplessly.

Gideon gave me my freedom…then threw me away before I could make my choice. But I would have stayed. I would have *stayed*.

And he never gave me a chance to tell him.

I cry until I'm spent, then lie there shuddering on the floor, all of my strength gone and my body as limp as a rag doll's.

I don't know where I find the willpower to get up again. But it must be from the same place where I find the resolve to unpack all of the clothes in my suitcase and put them away in my wardrobe again. And it must be where I find the steel that stiffens my spine and lifts my chin, and sends me in search of Gideon.

Because I *am* staying.

And if he doesn't believe it today, then he will fifty years from now, when I'm still right here.

In bare feet, I cross the grand hall and climb the stairs to the southeast tower. He's not there. Wishing I had a golden chain to follow, I head back downstairs and slip through the corridor to the family wing. In the parlor, everything is quiet.

Except for the low groan that faintly sounds from farther within the wing—from the direction of Gideon's bedchamber.

Heart pounding, I make my way to that room. The lamps are off and the curtains pulled, but orange light spills through the broken doorway to the solarium. Beyond those glass walls, the setting sun is but a sliver of gold leaving behind a blood-red sky.

"Cora? God, no. Cora." So guttural and thick, Gideon's voice is almost unrecognizable. *"Run."*

I did that last time. This time I go to him, to where he's crouched beside his bed, his shoulders hunched and his bare skin bathed in the sunset's flaming light.

"Gideon? What are you—" I stop dead, shock rooting me to the spot. He's been chained to the bed, but not with a thin golden chain. Instead it appears as if the heavy rusted chain from the manor's main gate has been padlocked around his waist. "Oh my god. Let me get you out! Who did this?"

"*I* did this." A warning growl rumbles from him, and he catches my frantic hands, stopping me from pulling at the chain wound around the solid oak frame. His intense green eyes demand my full attention. "I knew you must still be here, because I was not... You have to *run*, Cora. Through the solarium and outside, as fast as you can. You have to make it past the gates before the sun sets, because that's when the full moon will rise."

Determinedly I shake my head. I have no idea what's happening here, but I am not abandoning him to *this*, whatever it is. Because suddenly I remember his terrible gift, the one where he left Blackwood Manor to me... because something might happen to him. "I'm not leaving you behind. So tell me where the padlock key is."

"Cora. My beautiful Cora." Stark agony draws his features into a bleak emotional wasteland. "This chain will not hold me. It might slow me but a minute."

"But—"

His gaze darts toward the solarium. Anguish whitens his lips, rasps through his voice. "It's setting. Swear to me you'll run and you won't look back. Swear to me."

"I *won't* swear." Despair trembles through my voice. Whatever is about to happen, I can't leave him here alone. He's been alone for too long. "Where's the key to the padlock? Please come with me. *Please.*"

Abruptly he curls forward, every muscle in his body

straining. "Run," he growls again. *"RUN!"*

That...was not his voice. That was not *any* man's voice.

Fear suddenly pushes me back a step. I whisper uncertainly, "Gideon?"

"GO." It seems ripped from him, torn from his chest with jagged claws. *"DON'T...WATCH..."*

But I do. God help me, I do.

Stumbling back, I trip over my own feet and crash to the floor, but don't take my horrified gaze from the battle that seems to be taking place within Gideon's powerful body, muscles bulging outward as if caught in an explosion barely contained by his skin. I scream as his bones crack, reaching for him, trying to help him—then scrambling back when his head jerks up, his attention drawn by the sound of my cry. Sharp teeth gleam from a distending jaw, thick fur sprouting over smooth tanned skin.

Ohmygod, *ohmygod*. I know what this is. And it can't be real. *Can't* be.

But the full moon is rising. And somehow this is really happening.

So I better do what he says and run for my life.

Lurching to my feet, I race for the solarium—and stop, turning back for a last look. But it's not Gideon in that bedchamber anymore. Instead the werewolf is slowly rising onto his hind feet...rising and rising, taller than Gideon, at least a foot and a half taller than anyone I've *ever* seen, gray fur stretched taut over a body thick with muscle. Too strong to be stopped by that chain.

My gaze drops to his waist but it's not the chain or padlock I see. Only an enormous cock, fully erect, too utterly huge to be real.

But *all* of this is real.

The beast turns. Eyes as green as spring grass lock on my face. With a hungry growl, he takes a long step toward me—and is brought up short by the rusted chain.

On his next step, wood shrieks over stone as the beast drags the heavy oak bed with him.

I turn and flee.

His thunderous roar follows me.

Outside the sky is still a reddish orange on the western horizon, with just enough light to see by as I race down the slope outside the solarium—heading for the east access gate with the gap just wide enough to slip through. It's closer than the main gates and the grove might offer some protection and a place to hide if the beast escapes more quickly than I can run to the estate's border.

The distant shattering of glass warns me that he's made it through the solarium. Hopefully still dragging that bed, slowing him down.

I run like I've *never* run before, flying alongside the gravel walk, my sprinting feet flinging mud and sod, gaze fixed ahead—my mind racing as fast as my legs.

A werewolf. For how long?

But I know. I know. Because I've ran toward this gate before—but Gideon was beside me then. And he made certain that I went through first, that I was safe. But his leg was bleeding. I thought he'd cut it while struggling his way through the gate, but it must have been a bite or a scratch.

How does it spread? A curse? A disease? It seems like I've seen movies and read horror novels with both.

A howl pierces the night—not far behind me. I burst out of the grove of trees and onto the sprawling lawn. The moon rises full in the eastern sky, just above the horizon. Lungs burning, I draw upon all of my strength, all of my speed. A thousand yards directly ahead is the wall and the access gate that leads to safety.

Safety from a cursed beast.

It *has* to be a curse. Some kind of magic. Because a disease, that's logical, that's *science*—and there was nothing logical about the golden chain that bound me. That was magic, too. And it shouldn't have been real, either. But that chain undeniably was.

And it was magic that could be broken. Because Gideon removed the chain from my neck, knowing the danger that was coming with the full moon. And he tried to send me away. To save my life.

Then why the hell did he keep asking me to marry him? To allow him the use of my cunt for his pleasure? Because if I'd married him, if I'd taken him into my bed, I would have been here at the manor when the full moon rose. I would have been in danger on this night.

Except…curses can be broken, too.

Almost of their own volition, my feet slow. But it's

only my racing mind that is slow to catch up with what my pounding heart has already decided.

Because that beast looked at me with eyes as green as spring. That was Gideon, trapped inside that monster. And if I'm right, then I have the power to free him. He's told me how, almost every single night.

But I don't think this beast will ask me to marry him.

I also suddenly hope that he really does drag that bed all the way out here with him.

He hasn't.

I'm facing him, with my back to the rising moon, when he silently emerges from the grove, moving so swiftly that even if I hadn't stopped, I don't know if I would have made it to the gate.

But he slows now, too—perhaps confused that I've stopped. Or Gideon is fighting him.

I hear my name carry across the distance on a tortured growl. "CO…RA…"

Gripping the bottom edge of my T-shirt, I pull it over my head.

Immediately the tortured growl deepens hungrily. He's so close now, so utterly huge, thick furred shoulders like a mountain approaching, green eyes glowing with feral light.

His massive cock points straight at me. And magic or not, there is just *no damn way* that'll ever work. I couldn't even fit my mouth around it without unhinging my jaw, and unless a weresnake is coming along soon, that's not likely to happen, either. So I pray he can find his pleasure another way.

Fingers shaking, I unbutton my jeans. I don't even try to attempt a sexy tease, because he's almost upon me and I've never felt less sexy. So I shove the denim and my panties down my legs and turn my back to the beast, sinking onto my knees in the soft grass, bending over to brace my weight on my hands.

In a rush, I say, "I offer you the use of my cunt for your pleasure," and close my eyes, waiting.

Waiting. My nipples hard with fear and cold, my skin a tight, prickly ache. Waiting. As the whisper of steps over the grass and the heat radiating against the back of my legs tell me he's so close. Waiting. As his hot breath skims the curve of my ass and his soft growl fills the spring night.

Waiting…and wondering if I've misjudged everything and am about to be ripped apart.

I struggle to contain my whimper as clawed hands grip my hips, the razored tips gently pricking my skin. But I can't contain my cry of surprise as a long, hot tongue licks straight up my center.

Shock lurches me forward but he brings me right back with a warning growl that deepens on another lick. Heat blooms through my pussy and I'm shaking uncontrollably, everything within me at war. Another long, long lick has me dropping forward onto my elbows, then his rumbling groan sounds from behind me, and I know that sound, recognize Gideon's ravenous pleasure, the same as he made the night in his tower and in my bed today, as he lapped the juices from my cunt.

Now I moan his name as I press back against him. "Gideon."

Relentlessly he continues, taking his pleasure in the taste of my pussy and forcing my pleasure from me, rhythmically thrusting his rough tongue past my entrance as if to gather all of the honey from my inner walls, then flicking at my clit until I'm fisting my hands in the grass and crying out in delirious ecstasy. And with Gideon, I could push him away when it became too much, when the pleasure was too acute, but now the clawed hands hold me tighter and draw orgasm after orgasm from my body, pulling me taut across a rack of pleasure, until I simply give out and collapse onto my stomach in the grass, too utterly wrecked to support my own weight on my knees.

But he has not finished. The grip on my hips tightens. He lifts me up onto my knees again, higher, and I feel the hot, thick press of his massive cock against my virgin entrance.

And that is just *not* going to work.

Though he tries, steadily increasing the pressure, trying to push his way in—then we both groan when his enormous length slips forward through my drenched folds, riding across oversensitive bud of my clit.

Despite my body's exhaustion, my pussy clenches greedily, aching for more, aching to be filled. Panting into the fragrant grass beneath my cheek, I rock my hips back against him, and realize that I'd forgotten the other part of this. Because it wasn't simply allowing him the use of my cunt—I was to do it with love.

So as he fits the thick head of his cock to my entrance again, growling in deepening frustration, I softly breathe the words that have always lived in my heart.

"I love you, Gideon."

CHAPTER 4

Gideon

I LOVE YOU, GIDEON.

All at once, I sense everything. The ragged pass of Cora's breath between her trembling lips. The scalding pleasure of her cunt against the tip of my cock. The flex of her hips beneath my hands, the softness of her skin dimpling against my claws. The sweet scent of her arousal filling my lungs and her delicious flavor lingering upon my tongue.

Her cheek is pillowed against the grass, her hands fisted as she softly pants. Her hair is a pale tangle, her spine a long, elegant line leading to the beautiful swell of her ass. Against the soft pink flesh of her pussy, my painfully throbbing cock is slick with her honey and my pre-cum, and looks the size of a battering ram.

I'm wearing the wrong skin. The hunter's skin. The protector's skin.

I shed my beast form as easily as I would a shirt. No cracking of bone and agonizing shear of flesh. I don't know why the difference. But I know it's *right*.

As right as the way Cora feels against me.

Her pussy glistens with need, the pink flesh still swollen with arousal after my endless feast. Fisting my cock, I glide the thick crown the length of her slit, yearning to breach her virgin entrance and finally claim her. But not yet.

Bending over her, I press a kiss to the nape of her neck. "My beautiful Cora."

Her eyes fly open and energy surges through her languid form. Pushing up on her elbows, she looks back over her shoulder, a trembling smile on her lips. "Gideon?"

In answer I sit back on my heels and draw her up against my chest until she's straddling my thighs. Angling my head, I capture her mouth with mine. Eagerly she returns my kiss, her eyes swimming with tears, her joy so sweet that I can taste it, smell it.

Her love so deep that it's given me everything. Yet if I take her now, she will give me even more.

Releasing her lips, I press a kiss to the side of her neck. "The perfume of your arousal is ripe and fertile, Cora. If I come inside you tonight, the bond between us will be stronger than any golden chain, because you will carry my child."

Her breath shudders, and she rolls her hips back against my stiffened cock, as if already seeking my seed. "Yes. Do it."

As she demands. Bending her forward, I brace my left hand on the ground as my right locks her against me, my forearm angling up between her breasts and my fingers lightly clasping her throat, my thumb nestled in the hollow of her jaw.

Finally mounting her—and taking her on the ground, though she is an innocent who deserves a bed and gentleness. An hour ago, I would have blamed the beast within me. But there is only me. There's only *ever* been me. The beast and I were never any different.

And I am claiming my bride. Here, now.

She gasps when my burning erection lodges against her slick entrance, then moans, biting her lip as her untried flesh stretches to accept the broad head of my cock, her velvet inner walls giving way beneath the unyielding pressure. Groaning with pleasure, I thrust deeper, the faint copper scent of her virginity mixing with the heady fragrance of her nectar. Sweetly she cries out as I bury my full length deep inside the voluptuous clasp of her sheath, her back arching, her hips rising as if to escape my possession.

Then sliding back down, taking all of me again, her slippery juices easing the way.

The pulse in her throat races against my palm. Reaching back, she grasps a fistful of my hair. "Harder now," she moans. "I want all of you, Gideon."

She will have me.

With a thick growl, I surge my hips forward. She cries out again in helpless ecstasy, her pussy gripping every thick inch of my cock. I fill her again and again, and her cries become frantic pleas as I ruthlessly use her cunt for my pleasure…and hers. Her wetness drips between her thighs, my shaft glistening with her honey, and when she comes on a scream, her inner walls clamping down, I can't hold back anymore. With a guttural roar, I bury my cock deep, my hot cum spurting into her clenching sheath, filling her with a molten flood of seed.

Mine. Always mine. Forever bound to me.

Chest heaving, I pull her up and she sags back against me. "I can't," she pants breathlessly. "I can't come again."

I won't force her to, then. Not for another hour, at least.

My cum spills down her inner thighs as I slowly withdraw, but before she can reach for her clothing to wipe it away, I swing her up against my chest. Cradling her against me, I start off toward the manor house.

Toward home.

In the moonlight, her pale hair is silver. Her blue eyes shine with love as she gazes up at me, her swollen lips forming a soft, shy smile.

Then curving downward, her brow creasing.

I will allow nothing to mar her happiness. "What?"

"Your teeth," she says quietly, her lips quivering. "You still have fangs."

So I do. But they are already gone. "I will keep them

small, if they displease you."

"Displease…?" Confusion forms a furrow between her eyebrows. "No. But I thought we broke the curse."

"There is no breaking it," I say gruffly. "There is no cure."

And I would not want it if there was. Unless Cora asked it of me. Because a cure now would be like ripping away half of my soul.

But I would sacrifice that for her.

"Then…what happened? How did you fight free of the beast and gain control?"

"Because there's nothing to fight now. I *am* that beast. I always have been." I struggle to explain what I don't understand myself. But it is what I *know*. "We shared a heart and soul. And it was as if we were two halves of a whole with a rift between us. But you healed that rift. Now we are not two halves. Just a whole."

She gazes silently at me for a long time. "That's a little weird."

Only a little? But I nod.

"But so are magical necklaces." Linking her arms around my shoulders, she smiles up at me. "The fangs were kind of sexy."

I grin.

"Maybe not *that* long," she says, then laughs in delight when I shrink them again. "Now ask me."

My voice thick with emotion, I do as she says. "Will you marry me, Cora?"

Her blue eyes are solemn. "If I say yes, will you ever

let me go?"

"No," I vow.

"Then yes," she says, smiling happily.

"I love you, my beautiful Cora," I growl softly, then capture that smile in a heated kiss.

And far less than a hour passes before she comes again.

EPILOGUE

Cora

Fourteen months later, the first day (and night) of summer...

SILVER LIGHT FROM THE FULL moon shines through our bedchamber windows as I lie half-asleep in bed, awaiting Gideon's return—until sleep deserts me completely when plaintive cries sound from the nursery.

Since the date of his birth—which came a month early, on the night of the winter solstice—our son has never had a good sense of timing.

Smiling, I wrap a silk robe around my nude body and slip through the door to the adjoining chamber. The glow of a nightlight offers gentle illumination—and a view of the eight-foot-tall werewolf bending over the crib, with a dark-haired baby protectively cradled in one giant clawed hand.

"Just because our son is crying doesn't mean he's hurt," I tell the beast. "So you can stand down. It's probably a wet nappy. Or he's hungry."

Those vivid green eyes narrow on my breasts. His wolfish grin exposes razor-sharp teeth.

"Bad beast," I tease him, and gently lift Lucas out of his arms, turning toward the changing table. "He needs a new diaper. But you probably already smelled that."

His rumbling growl holds the sound of a laugh, and he edges in close behind me as I tend to the baby. His enormous form radiates heat like a furnace against my back, his breath hot over my skin as he bends to lick my neck.

"Behave," I whisper, even as shivers of pleasure race through me.

He behaves until I lay the sleeping baby down in the crib, then his big hands roughly grip my hips from behind and pull me back against his thickly furred chest. Through the thin silk between us, his steely arousal is a massive burning length against my back, *too* massive, yet the beast still takes what he wants, tearing aside the robe and sliding his hand into wetness and heat, the rough pads of his fingers rubbing over my sensitive clit.

Clinging to his forearm, I gasp out his name. "Gideon."

His answer is a ravenous growl, and he swings me up against his broad chest.

My breath coming in ragged pants, I tell him, "Put

me down."

His snarl draws his lips back over gleaming teeth.

"Put me down," I say again. "Then you can chase me."

Because his beast *loves* that. And I love what happens when Gideon catches me.

Though they *are* the same man. This I know with a certainty through to my bones. They have the same heart, the same soul. Whatever the beast is, he's not something that came from outside of Gideon. Instead it was a part of Gideon that was unleashed.

Still, the beast that he is never relinquishes me easily. This time he sets me on my feet for only a moment before he grips my waist and easily lifts me straight up into the air, thick muscles bulging in his shoulders and arms, my body dangling in front of him. Through a haze of arousal, I look down at those shining green eyes—and at that wolfish grin as he nuzzles the glistening curls between my thighs.

And he licks. And licks. And licks, his rough tongue slipping through my drenched folds and over my swollen clit, over and over, until I'm muffling my screams of ecstasy against my hands and writhing helplessly against him. Only after I come does he slowly lower me to my feet again, my legs trembling and aftershocks quaking through my body.

Then he growls against my ear, *"Run, wife."*

I do, racing for our bedchamber—and I know he gives me a head start. Just as he often used to when we raced as children. But he doesn't let me win.

Instead he catches me as I leap onto the bed, the beast in midair but it's Gideon who comes down over me. I land on the mattress breathless and laughing…then moaning in sheer ecstasy when he spreads my thighs and his rigid cock pushes deep inside me, his thickness stretching the taut inner walls of my sheath.

"Gideon," I breathe, and when he kisses me I taste my own desire on his tongue, taste the cold night and the moonlight and the feral fire that burns within his wild heart. My husband, my beast.

And in his arms is the place I'll always call home.

END

ABOUT THE AUTHOR

KATI WILDE IS A TIGHT-LIPPED, loose-hipped woman of indeterminate age and low breeding. Born into a very large family, she now has a very small family, and she writes romantic fiction to assuage her darker urge to write Transformers erotica. She lives in Oregon and has two old cats.

You can contact Kati by email at kati@katiwilde.com, on Facebook at facebook.com/authorkatiwilde/ or on Twitter at twitter.com/katiwilde. Find a list of all her books and upcoming works at www.katiwilde.com.